A gift to my neighbours!
If you like it drop me an email:

joff@jonathanleeauthor.com

or better still review it on Amazon or
Goodreads.

Enjoy!
Love xx

331

Praise for M. Jonathan Lee

"Very cleverly done, and I guarantee you will want to re-read it again once you get to the end, and know the full story. The first 5* review I've given this year. A fantastic and brave story."

Andrew Webber, author

"Original and inspired. Excellent."

Milly Johnson, Sunday Times Bestselling author

"I listened to all of it, which these days I only do with books I don't want to put down...a very good writer and also darkly funny... all [the] characters came to life on the page."

Trisha Ashley, Sunday Times Bestselling author

"Totally absorbing. Another page turner."

Michael Fowler, author

"A Tiny Feeling of Fear" may well become your new favourite book. It certainly is mine."

Nick Jones, author

"…actually perfect."

Michael Carter, author

"The 'twist' at the end is believable but impossible to guess. Read this book."

Mark Jackson, author

"First class… an excellent book."
Kathryn Hughes, Sunday Times best-selling author

"Remarkable… an amazing story of family life."

Harry Dunn, author

"An excellent read."

Robert Weston, author

"Beautifully told delicate tale of loss, grief and guilt."

Bloomin' Brilliant Books book blog

"Lee has created perfect characters, surrounded by an intense, and at times chilling plot. Five Stars."

Whispering Stories book blog

"Beautifully written and absorbing. I highly recommend it."

Linda's Book Bag blog

"Amazing debut novel."

Secret Manda book blog

"I love books like this – there are so few books out there that I find genuinely creepy in this way, and I love it when I stumble across one."

Jo's book blog

"A fantastic book which is comparable to The Unlikely Pilgrimage of Harold Fry and Lost and Found. You should all go and buy it now!!"

Sheli Reads' blog

"Then BOOM, holy smoke the ending really wasn't what I was expecting. I'm not going to say anymore on that matter but it totally blew me away."

It's All About The Books blog

"Poignant, honest [with] a perfect plotline."

Belgian Reviewer blog

"Wow - this is such a beautifully written, powerful novel which, though not action-packed, really made me feel like I was inside the head of someone feeling so trapped and unhappy. It really spoke to me, and I feel that this is such an important book to read."

Laura, snazzybooks.com blog

"The writing flows from the page in terrific style – one of those books you live while you are reading it, and will stay with you when you are done... I am quite sad it is over."

Liz Barnsley, Goodreads

"Lee is a talented writer... he has developed a well-structured, compassionate and human writing style."

"Enthralling, intriguing and thoughtful."

"Poignant, emotive and thought provoking, all words that came into my head as I was reading 'drift stumble fall'."

"The Page is unlike anything that I've read before. Primarily a thriller, it's also a dark and witty tale, with possibly one of the most obnoxious and quite cruel lead characters that I've ever come across."

"...this book will have you wanting more, it will have you turning the pages and restless sleep till you finish. This is the first I have read of this author and now I NEED to have more!"

"I finished this reading it late last night and I am still reeling with emotions. I am still coming to terms with all and everything that is continually making connections in my head..."

This edition published | 2020

First published | 2020
1 2 3 4 5 6 7 8 9 10

Hideaway Fall publishing
BBIC S75 1JL UK
www.hideawayfall.com

ISBN | 978-0-9954923-5-6

Set in Century Schoolbook MT

Lyrics reproduced by kind permission of Tom McRae (c) and
(p) 2000 db records and 2005 (c) (p) Sony/atv Music Publishing
Limited ASCAP | Cover designed by Hot Frog
Original art by Paul Morton| 2020

Printed and bound by Charlesworth Press | 2020
Visit www.mjonathanlee.com | www.hideawayfall.com

331

a novel by m. jonathan lee

Light me a smoke
I'll tell you a story

I feed on fire and confusion
Of this crime I'll rid my soul
I told my troubles to the river
She shared them with the seas
She returned them to me doubled
The river holds no offer of peace

Like a snake eating snake you confuse me
Who's killer?
Who's captive?
Who's free?

– Tom McRae

Chapter 1

From a place high above the clouds, all you can make out is an expanse of green. The colour is deep, almost bottle, and from here it looks like the velvet upholstery of old dining chairs you'd find in a stately home or colonial house. It looks so soft you want to reach out and touch it. You want to push the brushed fabric in the wrong direction. Mess with its beauty.

As you pass through the wispy clouds (which persevere in trying to spoil the perfect summer's day) you can see that the ground beneath is actually covered in squares of varying colours and sizes. Blues and yellows and reds all thrown down haphazardly across the land, like playing cards in a game of pairs strewn across the floor. Each is different, yet each very much the same, and all are surrounded by an area of green before the next one begins.

As you drift closer, you can make out movement. At first you could be forgiven the triteness of using a word like 'ants' or 'insects' to describe them. But such nouns have been used to death by humans travelling on planes or hot air balloons or standing atop skyscrapers or whatever. By the time you have a chance to consider this, and indeed another noun, it is too late. It is clear that the grey, non-descript shapes – which move slowly, like oil in water – are humans. And lots of them.

You notice that the grey shapes are grouped together. They gather around the squares, and those without squares instead sit in circles. They walk in twos, in threes, in fours. Some move quickly; others, stretched out, long and thin, don't move at all.

You are getting close now, gently floating as carefree and relaxed as snow falling from a cottonwood tree. You are able to make out the scene beneath you more clearly. You can't yet see the faces of the people below, but you can make out their shapes. Their shapes and positions. Groups of people are gathering around what it is now clear are multi-coloured blankets, to eat in the open and celebrate the beauty of this near-cloudless day – to walk, to sit, to reflect, to play games, to talk, *to be human* and take in the warmth from the strange ball of fire which exists somewhere out there in the blackness of space and keeps them all alive.

Your eyes dart in all directions, naturally following sudden bursts of movement or unusually bright squares. You focus, but just for a moment, before something else catches your eye. The pattern repeats over and over, and you wonder what it is exactly that you are supposed to be looking for. And at the moment you wonder, it all becomes clear.

There are now less than thirty squares in your line of sight. They are laid out at different angles, some positioned as diamonds, others perfectly straight. Most are predominantly blue, red or green. Or a chequered combination of two, or all three.

One stands out from the rest.

A yellow blanket.

And that is the one you choose to focus on.

Soon, all you can see is the yellow blanket, surrounded by a moat of green, the edges of nearby blankets just encroaching on the edges of your peripheral vision.

Around the blanket you can see six people.

That's us.

Me and my family.

Just the six of us.

If you had joined us three years earlier, you would have also met my grandparents on my mother's side. But they've gone now.

So now there's just my remaining grandparents; then me, my mum, my dad and my brother.

From here, we are perfectly normal in every way. We look the same as the rest of those surrounding their squares today. We eat the same food. We breathe the same air. We share the same skies.

You couldn't tell from this snapshot that everything would be different for us. You wouldn't have guessed that within a day of this vision of warm cordiality my mother would disappear.

Like a puff of smoke.

Gone.

Chapter 2

We gather annually for the family picnic.

I am told that in years gone by up to thirty family members would attend. That was back in the days when most of the family lived on the streets of endless terraced houses which surround the park, all within a couple of doors of one another. They would gather on the first Sunday of July each year (which was the tradition, though nobody can now remember why) and eat, play games and spend time together.

I have a vague recollection of playing badminton in the humid, windless summer days when I was much younger. I remember large, park-wide games of hide and seek with perhaps twenty participants. But the day of the picnic that I am describing to you is far more mundane. Family members have long since given up making the effort to attend. Many have died (and therefore could be forgiven for their absence), whilst others simply didn't pass on the tradition to the next generation.

On that day, there are just six of us. I sit crossed-legged alongside my father on the west side of the blanket. My mother sits to the north, separated from my father by my younger brother, Tom, who is lying across my mother's outstretched legs. He is five years younger than me and rarely leaves my mother's side. It is almost as if he cannot function without some part of his body touching hers. My father says it is unnatural behaviour for a seven year old. My mother seems to like it. She props herself up with two straightened arms outstretched behind her.

Opposite me sits my gramma. The distance between her and the large wicker picnic basket suggests she is unduly worried that somebody may steal it or, worse still, open it without her say-so. Next to her (and thus next to me) at the south end of the picnic sits Gramps. His back is slightly turned to me, his brown polished shoes just encroaching on the blanket. He is wearing a full three-piece suit and tie. Sweat from his grey temples glistens in the sunshine.

"Are we actually going to eat today?" he barks, his question landing somewhere centrally between us all.

Gramma smiles warmly and begins unpacking the basket. Paper plates, plastic cups, knives and forks and all manner of items begin a circle from my gramma to my mother and so on, until I pass each item to my gramps. He doesn't acknowledge me, and instead of holding items up until my wrists hurt, I place his items in a small pile between us.

Gramma removes from the basket plates and bowls full of food, all held in place with tight cling film on which condensation has formed. Everything is spread out on the blanket in front of us: an array of sandwiches, sausage rolls, tomatoes, lettuce, vol-au-vents, crisps, celery, cheese, crackers. We wait patiently as she removes the cling film from each item. Gramps lights his pipe and we all wait a little longer until he has finished smoking. I watch the smoke disappear into the blue sky and wish for a moment it was me.

Eventually, Gramps collects his plate and begins to fill it with food. Again, we all wait, watching in silence until he has finished. Then he places his plate down on the grass next to him and bows his head solemnly. He closes his eyes and reopens them, and that is an indication that we can now join in.

I watch as Gramma fusses around, passing plates crammed with different food to each of us so we can fill our plates with what we wish. To break the silence, she insists on describing what is on each plate as we take it from her. My mother fills her own plate and one for my brother. She encourages him to sit up to eat. I notice her touch my gramma's hand and their eyes make contact for the shortest time. Then she pours diluted orange juice into the plastic cups that we each hold out. Except for Gramps.

I am about to bite into my sausage roll when I see my father's brow crease. He nods to divert my attention to Gramma, who at last is able to collect her own food from what is left. I place the sausage roll back on my plate and wait.

To my right, I hear Gramps chewing his food loudly. His teeth crunch and gnaw each mouthful as if there is a time limit until the food permanently disappears. I suppose in some ways it is. I hear the saliva clack-clacking between his cheeks and gums, in the spaces where his teeth used to be. I imagine tiny pieces of carrot being thrown from the top to the bottom of his mouth and back again, twisting and spinning on saliva rapids. I imagine it's like being in a kayak or on a waterslide.

He discards his empty plate, which lands on top of a bowl of luminous-orange cheesy crisps. He then lies back on the grass and places his cap over his face, exposing only his mouth, which turns down at the edges.

"Did you enjoy that, dear?" Gramma asks him.

"No. Too wet. Should've used foil."

I watch as Gramma smiles uneasily, her eyes flicking around all sides of the compass. Then she picks up a tomato, and I take my sausage roll and put it in my mouth just as she takes her first bite of the tomato. The silence is almost palpable, an invisible ghost that hovers above the blanket. I push food into my mouth, chewing as quietly as the scene around me. I'm not sure why we are all eating in silence. I suspect it is because Gramps is being silent. I chew on a small pork pie and realise that I am doing so in tandem with Gramps' chest inflating and emptying.

My father stretches and places his plate on the edge of the picnic blanket. A small gust of wind collects it and deposits it, upside down, in the salad bowl. He shrugs, perhaps to himself, and then lies back on the grass. His eyes are hidden by the crook of his elbow. His mouth reminds me of Gramps'.

Gramma nods and winks at me as she sucks on a mouthful of crisps. She looks grey. Grey and solemn. Her eyes remind me of the prisoners and refugees I have seen on the news. Eyes don't seem to shine when the hope is taken from them.

I notice a similar look on my mother's face. Her eyes crease when she sees me looking at her and a shy smile crosses her lips. I smile back broadly.

"What are you smiling at?" Tom asks loudly.

Gramma's head snaps toward him.

"Mum," I say quietly, hoping that Tom will take the volume hint (though he could be forgiven for his loud voice on the basis that he is in an expansive park full of hundreds if not thousands of people).

He doesn't. "Mum, Sam is pulling faces at me."

Mum frowns at me.

"Samuel," my father snaps.

Tom smirks.

I decide not to protest.

"So," says Gramma almost inaudibly, "any plans for this week, Sandra?"

"Not really," Mum says. There is a nervousness in her smile.

"Oh," says Gramma.

And then I am returned to the present. Completely aware of life around me. Suddenly, colours and sounds cascade from all directions. I hear the shouts of excitable children and the sound of bats hitting balls and, I hear laughter.

Laughter.

The ghost lifts from above the blanket, disappearing into the sky like chimney smoke. I see the brightness of the world come swiftly into focus. I see people smiling, running, talking. I see dogs eagerly taking in their surroundings, sniffing at trees, their tongues hanging in the summer heat. I see enjoyment.

I look around our blanket again. Tom has rested back on my mother's knees and she is playing idly with his hair as she stares above my shoulder and into space. Something tells me that she hasn't noticed the colours like I have. Dad and Gramps are breathing in warm air whilst dreaming about anything but the picnic. Gramma begins emptying half-eaten bowls of food into one another. Celery with tomatoes. Damp sausage rolls alongside cheese-and-pineapple sticks. Unfinished vol-au-vents crammed in with strategically broken breadsticks. And then our picnic blanket is empty. Just like our picnic.

Empty.

Empty of enjoyment. It's like a huge handful of happiness was sprinkled onto the park from above and somehow missed our blanket. Missed my family.

I lie back and let the summer sun warm my face, happy for one reason alone. That this event happens but once a year.

Chapter 3

It is the sound of my phone vibrating that wakes me from the dream about my mother and a picnic that happened almost exactly twenty-five years ago. I have had the same dream so many times that I have been able to pinpoint every moment of the day that the final picnic took place. In some ways it was easy to do. After all, I never saw my mother again after that day. You don't forget the details of days as significant as that.

I roll over to my right and watch the phone progress slowly over the edge of the bedside table. It swings for a moment, attached to its charging cable, and then hangs precariously like a mountaineer over a precipice.

I retrieve the still-vibrating phone and lie on my back. I push the button on the side and note that the caller is my father.

I could do without this.

The green circle allows me to answer, and am immediately greeted by the usual recorded message. I press '1' to accept and there are numerous clicks before his voice breaks through.

"Sam?" he says.

"Hi, Dad."

"How are you, son?"

"I'm good," I say. "And you?"

"Yeah. Y'know. I'm okay. Considering."

"Good."

Our conversations have always been much the same and now, in the position we both find ourselves, I have little hope that this will ever change. Even in the past – before my mother vanished – my father always kept our exchanges (and those with most other people) as short as possible. Our conversations almost exclusively serve as a way for my father to obtain information rather than share it. Today is different.

"Listen," he says, "your gramma hasn't got long left."

"Okay," I say, and before I can speak again, he interrupts my pause.

"Let's not pretend it matters to you," he says, quite rightly. "But she has no-one close, and well –"

It's my turn to interrupt. "So you think I should go and see her?"

"I'd do it myself..." he says. Neither of us feel the need to end his sentence. We both know why he can't. Doesn't.

My mind jumps to Tom.

My father tells me where my gramma is, which turns out to be only a mile or so from my home. You see, I was the one who stayed back. I was the one who stayed marooned in a broken town full of broken memories. Just in case Mum reappeared. You never know.

It seems that Gramma stayed too. But I didn't know that. I haven't spoken to her since I was eighteen. And that was nineteen years ago.

"So you will?" my father says.

"Dunno. Maybe," I say, the vagueness sounding far better in my head. It's my attempt at taking a little control back. If you had listened carefully you would have heard an uncertain tremor in my delivery.

"I suggest you do," he says in a voice which suggests there may be ramifications if I choose not to.

My only remaining thread of control is severed when he hangs up the phone. I take a deep breath and wait for him to call back, which is something he does when he feels he may not have made his point as clearly as he might. I lay there staring at the dust that has collected in the corners of my phone. The screen stays black, and after a minute or two passes I feel safe again. I place the phone on the duvet and turn my face into the darkness of the pillow.

For a moment I am gripped by anger, a feeling that twists in my chest like a coiled rope. I have spent a good part of the last ten years trying to remove this feeling from my life. I have been told on a number of occasions that if I cannot leave it behind, it will eventually consume me. I'll be tossed into the black hole of its throat like Jonah and his whale. Gobbled up in one. My final resting place will be the belly of the giant beast and, unlike Jonah, I'll never be seen again.

The last person who told me this was Sara. In fact, she told me plenty of times that I needed to change aspects of myself. For some time I listened to her, convinced that my macabre back story was reason enough to be the person I've become. It was only latterly, when I had an awakening, that I realised that her criticisms of me were actually a product of her own insecurities. Her insecurities moulding me into an angry and self-pitying person. A person I never used to be, nor ever wanted to be. And so, over the last year or so, the words I had listened to so attentively were rubberised and deflected, unheard, back to where they came from.

And of course, as I am sure you can now guess, Sara is gone.

And I feel the real me returning.

Slowly.

Chapter 4

I drink coffee until it's past lunchtime.

I lie stretched out on the sofa, my eyes closed, yet somehow staring far out into space. Someone rambles inanely on the radio in the background. My therapist says that it is good to just enjoy the moment. To breathe in the air (four seconds' deep breath in, three seconds' deep breath out, and repeat) so as to connect each of my senses with every aspect of what is around me. This is supposed to bring me into the moment. To stop me eternally procrastinating over what is coming next – a habit that comes from my past, I am told.

I take my breaths and try to focus, fighting off thoughts of what happens to the extra second of air that I breathe in each time. I push this and other random thoughts carefully to the perimeter of my mind.

I take in the smells: coffee. Last night's Indian.

I take in the sounds: radio babble that is just too quiet to hear properly but loud enough to irritate me. The cars passing on the road outside.

I disregard my sense of sight (my eyes are closed).

Taste: coffee, of course.

My sense of touch is taken up wholly by the heat from the mug which I hold between my hands, resting on my stomach.

I pause, for once able to empty my mind of everything. And then I realise that I've arrived. I am here. I am officially in the moment. At this moment I will take everything in. Everything.

I breathe back in, long and deep.

Coffee.

Onion bhajis.

Intermittent traffic noise and,

near-scalded hands.

I open my eyes. It's hardly a memorable moment.

It's not the type of moment that I can imagine retelling to a circle of wide-eyed grandchildren in the future. But, I tell myself, I was there. Just for the shortest of moments I was there, living it exactly how it was.

I get up from the sofa, quietly pleased that I somehow accessed a moment – something that my therapist and I have been working on for what seems like forever. As I pass through the hall, I nip into the kitchen and grab a Sharpie. Then I write in big letters on the back of an envelope: 'Lived in Moment'.

I don't want to forget to tell my therapist.

She'll be pleased.

I head upstairs to shower.

Chapter 5

As the shower water cascades down my back, I think of Tom.

You would expect that my brother and I would be close. After all, we should have both experienced the same levels of loss and childhood confusion. We both lost our mother. And losing her ultimately meant that we lost our father too. And our grandparents. And ultimately ourselves.

In fact, it was Tom who initially alerted me to her disappearance. I don't want to be cliched and tell you I remember it like it was yesterday because I don't. Too much has happened in between. But I do remember moments that somehow have become engrained in my mind and seem to take on great significance as individual threads in a much larger tapestry.

I remember lying on my front on my bedroom floor. I don't remember if I was building a Lego town that day or drawing. I suspect it was the latter. That was my usual way to lose a day. Though for the purposes of my story, I don't suppose it matters. My bedroom was the only one of the three that was at the back of the house. We lived in a small but nice detached house on the outskirts of a picturesque village surrounded by countryside. The city was a forty-five-minute drive away. Thankfully, the house was big enough for me and Tom to have our own rooms (I'm not sure that we would have lasted more than a few hours sharing).

My room looked over the back garden, which stretched around the side of the house in a typical L shape. From my window you could see to the top of the garden, where my dad had planted his rows of vegetables far out of the way, adjacent to the long hedge which separated us and the woods, and a thoroughfare known locally as Beggar's Path.

Down the left-hand side was an enormous row of conifer trees dividing our land from next door's. Although strictly our neighbours were next door, their house was well over half a mile away from ours.

Our garden dropped before the vegetable patch, with three steps down to a large area of grass and neatly tended flowerbeds. Three more steps led you onto the concrete flagged patio area and through the back door into the conservatory. There was a further entrance at the side of the house, leading into the kitchen.

I remember that morning, I heard my bedroom door open and I turned to see Tom coming in. He said that he had something to show me. I know that I turned away from him, back to what I was doing at the time. And then he appeared in front of me and whispered my name, and his face told me instantly that whatever it was I must go and look.

I remember the brightness of the sun streaming in through the landing window. Powerfully bright, to the extent that I had to follow Tom blindly down the stairs, covering my eyes with my hand, salute-style, as I walked. And then I remember the coldness hitting me as I turned out of the sun and down the second half of the split staircase, the back of my neck feeling cold as stone as I moved into the shadows.

Tom walked slowly and stopped at the kitchen door as if afraid to go any further. The sunlight from the window of the small cloakroom beneath my bedroom threw a long, thin triangle across the hall rug. In hindsight, you could say it provided the effect of an arrow pointing toward the truth.

Feeling Tom's fear, I stopped just behind him, using my height advantage to stare at the same thing that he was staring at. This proved difficult, as I didn't know what exactly he was staring at. The kitchen looked like it did most mornings. Clean, bright, tidy. My eyes scanned the work surfaces, which still looked slightly wet from whoever had wiped them down. Mum, of course. Cleaning wasn't Dad's thing. The sink was empty, a white dishcloth folded neatly and hanging like a tired ghost over the gleaming mixer tap. All the oat-coloured cupboard doors were closed both beneath and above the worktop. In the two frosted-glass cupboards on the wall on the far side, it was clear the crockery was neatly stacked diagonally in custom-made racks, as it always was. The wooden kitchen table sat in the middle of the room surrounded by six matching chairs, two at either side, one at either end. A bowl of fruit lay in the middle. This appeared to be where Tom was looking.

We both turned our heads at the same time and faced one another. Tom's mouth was already open. He must have clocked my facial expression because he spoke before I did.

"It's on the table," he whispered.

"What is?" I responded, craning my neck to see over the kitchen chairs.

He turned away and courage took him the few paces to the table. I followed.

"This," he said.

On the table lay two rings. I noticed one had a diamond. The other was a simple gold band. A near-blank piece of paper (partially screwed up before being flattened out again) lay next to the rings. In black typewriter text, across the middle and slightly off-centre, read the following:

Ray
I've left you. Look after the boys.
Sandra

I picked up the paper and turned it over to make sure that it had no further clues on the reverse. It didn't.

"What does it mean?" Tom asked, his eyes wide.

I shook my head. I didn't know. It was clear the note was from my mother to my father. It seemed to mean that she had left. But, I supposed, it could mean anything. I picked up the rings and moved them around my palm. They looked like my mum's rings, but I couldn't be sure. I could be sure she had one with a clear-glass-coloured stone and one without because I'd seen them on the windowsill before when she cleaned the bathroom. I let the two rings dance in my palm, enjoying the clinking sound they made while I tried to think.

I turned to Tom, who looked like he was about to cry. "I don't know, Tom," I said. "Let's find Dad."

We were around the house in a matter of seconds. In and out of every room, shouting for our father. When we returned to the kitchen, we decided to go around again, just in case. This search was more thorough and I am sure we ended up shouting "Dad!" into wardrobes and cupboards and cubby-holes into which he couldn't possibly fit. At that moment, though, I remember nothing making any sense.

We pulled on our shoes and rushed out onto the drive. Tom followed my lead and together we raced around the side of the house and into the back garden. We shouted out for Dad again, but it was clear he wasn't there. We went up the steps to the top of the garden, just in case.

And then we returned to the front of the house at lightning speed. I think I was hoping that when we arrived I'd see my mum and dad pulling into the drive and everything would be okay.

And then it struck me: the car.

It wasn't there.

Tom and I were standing where the car should be.

If the car wasn't there,

then neither was Dad.

I remember just standing there, thinking that it was far too bright outside for anything bad to happen.

Chapter 6

I lie down on the bed, the towel wrapped around me. I can feel drips of water running from my hair and down the back of my neck. I pick up my phone, hold it for a few seconds and then replace it on the bed beside me. It isn't often nowadays that I contact Tom. In fact, I'm not sure if I even have the right number for him.

Everybody has a limit, a point where they have reached capacity on a given experience, whether it be revising for exams or suffering daily abuse from a bully. Eventually, the person simply cannot take anymore. In some ways it is similar to the moment when the love you should feel for your family dries up. The open expressions of love begin to heal over, like a scab, until the emotion is no longer visible. And ultimately, when the dry scab peels away, the love is gone.

This is especially true for a sibling. Too many things happen which make you come to the conclusion that if the sibling was one of your friends then you would simply unfriend them. With a sibling instead you begin to distance yourself from the choices they make – probably embarrassed that someone who swims in the same gene pool can make such catastrophically bad decisions.

This began for Tom when he was around thirteen. Until then he had coped as well as could be expected with the forced changes in our family unit. After that… well, I'll tell you some other time.

I scroll through my phone and bring Tom's name into view. I tap the screen and put the phone on speaker mode. There is something that makes me feel less close, less connected with him if he's not speaking directly into my ear.

The phone goes to voicemail. I check the time. It's after two in the afternoon. It should be a reasonable time to call. Before I can put the phone down again, it rings.

"Sam, s'up?" he says drowsily. Barely audible.

I tell him to speak up.

"Sorry, man, late one. Y'know how it is."

I don't.

I notice his voice sounds ragged, as if the muscles in his neck have been stretched so far as to be torn. Like he is speaking through a throatful of glass.I tell him of the situation with Gramma. He doesn't ask how I know. He punctuates the end of my sentences with the word 'shit'. Anyone listening in may be tricked by his fake empathy and believe that, even for a second, he cares.

"So, you gonna come up and see her?" I say.

There is a pause, and I hear him take a drink.

"I dunno, maaan," he says, stretching out his literal definition of my gender to a length that is far more than just annoying.

"What do you mean?"

"I dunno. Not got much time right now, to be honest."

I'm instantly suspicious of anyone who has to clarify the veracity of a statement with words like 'to be honest' or 'I want to be totally/brutally honest now' – the inference being that most of the other times they've spoken, they've not been truthful. I ignore Tom's use of the words.

"Not much time?" I try not to sound accusatory. Though I don't remember Tom ever having a job of any kind.

"Nah, was out last night. You heard of Neil Young?"

"Yeah, 'course."

"Went to see him last night. Hung out with him after the gig." He coughs, and then I hear the click of a lighter. He breathes in smoke. "Jammed a bit. He liked some of my stuff."

"You jammed with Neil Young?"

"Yeah, backstage, man," he says.

"Like, Neil Young? Legend Neil Young?"

"Yeah. It was fucking wild. Drinks. Smokes, y'know..."

My brother. Professional mythomane. I wonder if he believes for one moment the words he is saying. I wonder whether he is so distant from the rest of us that he cannot tell that the words he is using are lies. I cannot understand how he can just let them flow from his mouth. I blame my father, partially.

"Right," I say.

"So, y'know, need to stay close to where the shit happens. Ear to the ground, y'know."

"You made plans to see Neil again?" I say, just managing to sand off the roughness of any sarcasm.

"Dunno. He's over with some US band who are playing for four nights."

"Who are they?" I ask.

"No idea. Some small-band-gonna-be-big thing."

It's a convenient answer.

"Listen, gotta go, Sam. Good to talk."

The line goes dead.

And that's it.

The responsibility for Gramma's final earthly moments is to fall on me. It is what I expected, though. It is no surprise that the only two surviving members of my family (my dad had Mum pronounced dead back in '99, just in time for the millennium) will leave it to me to carry the burden. As usual. As has always been the case.

As I dress, I wonder what would happen if I too decided not to visit Gramma. What if I decided that I couldn't be bothered to make the effort? If I decided that instead of seeing my dying relative, I would pursue the imaginary possibility of playing music with a world-renowned rock star?

And it instantly comes to me.

Nothing would happen.

Nothing at all.

Gramma would die.

Alone.

And the impact on my life would be the same as removing one grain of sand from the Sahara.

But there is something that makes me different to my brother, my father. It is more than just a yearning not to be like them. It is actually a part of me. A part of what makes me the way I am. I am not like them. I have always played this role. I've spent a lifetime making up for their behaviour by doing more than one person could ever be reasonably expected to do.

To be honest with you, Gramma dying alone doesn't even bother me.

After what happened, it's no more than she deserves.

I make my way downstairs into the kitchen and click on the kettle. I try to imagine how I would have felt if my father had called and told me that Gramma had already died. I concentrate, stripping away my personal feelings for her and wrestling with how I should feel on hearing of the death of anybody. I am still thinking as the rush of steam is propelled into the underside of the kitchen cupboards, dispersing in all directions like the mushroom from an atom bomb.

I decide that I will make the effort and at least visit her once.

That feels right.

I'll do it tomorrow.

As I walk through the hallway with my coffee, I can distinctly hear my mother. Today, the sound is quiet, almost inaudible, and I stop dead to ensure I don't miss even a breath. I wonder whether, if I didn't live alone now, my wife would hear her. She never mentioned hearing her whilst we were together, but I wouldn't expect her to, especially as she wouldn't know how my mother sounded. I never mentioned it either. I suppose it's just, well, something you don't bring up in everyday conversation.

Now I am still, it is a little easier to make out her voice. The sound is quiet, yet joyful like a gospel choir. My mother sings in the same way that she used to do when cleaning or polishing when I was so much younger. I remember sitting on the stairs listening to her sugary voice fill the hallway and watching her through the wooden balustrades as she punctuated notes with her duster or a hoover attachment.

I can't quite make out the song she is singing. Sometimes her voice is crisp and clear and I instantly recognise the song. Today, I can just about hear the melody, but her voice is drowned out by a sound similar to static.

I remain statuesque and listen anyway, desperate to somehow wipe away the crackles and pops from the surface of the record so I can hear her clearly. From time to time, a single word bursts through the static and momentarily I hear her voice as if she is standing right behind me. Her voice is honey and candyfloss and golden syrup and sweet tea. It is clean as cotton and fresh as toothpaste. It is soft and clear, and sounds like purity itself.

Chapter 7

I wake earlier than I usually would on a Sunday.

My sleep has improved enormously over the last few months, but this morning I'm awake long before the sunrise. I lie in bed, listening to the rain hit the aging tiles on the roof above. I'd like to be able to tell myself that it was the rain that woke me, but I know deep inside that it was the day ahead that woke me. The rain was simply there to greet me.

There is something comforting about hearing rain fall just a few feet away from you, yet not getting wet. There is a feeling of protection, that nothing outside can hurt you. That you are safe. Well, I think so anyway.

I stare at the closed window blind, just able to make out the shadow of the sky outside. It is, predictably, grey, and I decide to leave the blind closed in a vain attempt to not acknowledge what is happening outside. It's like if I don't actually see the weather, it may be different from what I expect. It's another trick that I've learned from my therapist. Try not to spend time predicting situations ahead. Live for now. This very moment.

I lie there for a few hours in what turns out to be a mixture of simply staring, reading the news on my phone and focusing my thoughts to hold back a torrent of ruminations which threaten to flood my mind. The latter proves to be difficult, and I allow myself to satiate some of my thoughts. After all, I am about to spend a day with a dying relative whom I haven't seen for nearly twenty years. The time that has elapsed since we last spoke should give you an indication that issues exist in our relationship. It should be evident that we are not close. I'll be surprised if she even recognises me.

After breakfast and a shower, I am finally ready to dress for my visit. It takes me at least half an hour to choose what to wear. I have a clear memory that Gramma would always comment on my appearance. My hair not tidy enough. My shirt not tucked in. Her dislike of my ripped jeans.

A part of me wants to pull on clothes she wouldn't approve of. Just to show her that I am my own person and I make my own choices. I consider and then reconsider t-shirts for being the wrong colour (lemon or pink on a man?) or for displaying a band logo that may offend her (God forbid a t-shirt with a crucifix or skull). I know that her ideal would be a smart shirt and tie, trousers, shoes and perhaps a blazer to finish.

I meet her somewhere between with a black collarless t-shirt covered by a black woollen jumper and dark jeans. Plain black trainers is the closest I can get to the footwear she'd like to see me in.

It'll have to do.

Whatever I wear will not suit her.

I pull on my black rain jacket and close the front door behind me. The sky has taken on a lilac hue which doesn't look real. It feels like a purple filter has been applied to the world around me. The clouds look heavy, ready to shed their weight. For now, though, the rain has stopped, and I unzip my jacket and pull my hood back down.

The walk to the nursing home will only take me half an hour. I walk quickly, past the large Victorian houses which line each side of the wide road. Short driveways climb steeply to oversized glass-panelled wooden front doors. Most of the houses are lit from inside, as if to fight off the darkness of the day outside. Vast sycamore trees suck the pavement up towards the sky like mythical beanstalks spurting from beneath the road. Aside from the irregular crunch of a small branch or twig beneath my feet and the dripping of water, the day is soundless.

I check my watch and am surprised that it is nearly eleven. It seems that the rest of the world has decided to stay indoors today. The quietness is eerie. I increase my walking speed, wondering for a short moment whether the rest of the world knows something I don't (there didn't seem to be anything on the news).

I am happy to finally see the sign for the nursing home on my left-hand side. I cross over the road and stand at the end of the drive for a moment. The sign is large and painted white, with black lettering. The letters have a gold shadow which gives them a three-dimensional look. I've arrived.

St Dymphna's Nursing Home.

I take a picture of the sign with my phone and then make my way up the steep path to the dark-looking building that sits high above the roadside.

As I approach the wide steps that lead to the front door I hear a loud crack, which makes me jump slightly. By the time I reach the top of the steps heavy rain has burst from the clouds and is falling against a backdrop of electricity, which fizzes and flashes and turns the sky every shade of purple.

Chapter 8

There is a buzzer on the door, which, as instructed by the small handwritten card inside the glass, I push. I can vaguely hear a rattling sound inside the building. The chime of the bell is now a simple rattle. It seems ironic that even the building is getting too old to function.

While I wait, I peer through the glass window. Inside is a short corridor leading to a space at the foot of a wide staircase which disappears out of sight. The building is old and the ceilings high. Along the corridor are various doors, some open, some closed.

Eventually, I hear a click and I push the door open. It sticks to the frame and I struggle through. As I close the door behind me, I am instantly greeted by a small man who appears from my left from what looks like a small office. All manner of papers and boxes fill the room. On the desk opposite the open door is a monitor which seems to be showing live angles of the building, both inside and outside, on a continuous loop. The monitor is framed by a hundred colourful Post-it notes and adhesive arrows.

The man smiles. He is dressed all in white and reminds me of a nurse. His badge tells me he is Tony.

"Can I 'elp you?" he says. It is clear from his accent that he isn't a Tony. Perhaps an Antonio or Anton. Maybe at a stretch a Gaston. He sounds Eastern European and my best guess is Albanian.

"Hi, er, yeah, I'm here to see my gramma."

He frowns and I see suspicion in his eyes.

"I'm here to see Joan. Joan Rose Darte."

"You are?" he says. I notice he is yet to blink.

"I'm her grandson, Sam," I say.

"Okay," he says and turns. "Come."

I follow behind as we make the short journey past three more doors to the bottom of the stairs. Two of the doors are closed. One is open. I see a bed, covered with a thick blanket. Its inhabitant faces away from me towards a window. I can just make out a nest of grey hair on the pillow. It is tangled like it has been removed from a hairbrush.

Tony stops at a small table and bends to leaf through a landscape leather-bound book. I stand behind him, noticing for the first time that a thin layer of ginger and white hair covers the top of his head and seems to form a canopy over his pale skin. It reminds me of smoke on a Lowry. At the sides, above his ears, the hair is much thicker. Twisted rust.

He stands and moves to one side. "Sign, please."

I fill in the date, my name and who I am visiting in bold capitals. I can feel him watching. I straighten and turn to him, smiling.

"Mrs Joan, she never mention grandson," he says.

I raise my eyebrows, unhappy with his inference that I may not be who I say I am. I leave his statement hanging for a moment as my eyes follow the vast staircase, which stretches at least three storeys. I wonder where in the building she is.

"Come," he says again.

We snake through corridors, past endless closed doors, each displaying a number and a printed name placard. Tony stops abruptly, and I am lucky not to collide with him. He turns to his right. "Mrs Joan," he says. "Wait."

He knocks on the door lightly and enters without waiting for a response. The door closes behind him. I am left looking at a high-gloss white door with the number 4 and my gramma's full name in capitals.

A few moments pass, then the door opens again and Tony stands with his back against it, waving me through with a flick of his hand. I step inside, the door closes again and I am left, seemingly alone, in a long, narrow room with a large window at the far end.

On my left is a small shower room which shares a wall with the bed where my Gramma must sleep. Against the pink-velour headboard she has three pillows, plumped so tall that they nearly touch the wedding picture which hangs above. It appears that Gramps was unable to smile on that day too.

I notice an opened bag of Murray Mints on her bedside table, along with a few books and a lamp. At the end of the bed is a television sitting atop a chest of drawers which I recognise from years before.

There is a large, high-backed chair which faces the window. Various family photographs line the windowsill. Next to the window, an old-fashioned-looking wardrobe stares ominously down the room. I recognise the wardrobe too.

As I reach the back of the chair, my pocket vibrates and I pull out my phone. It's my dad. I switch the phone to silent and replace it in the darkness of my pocket. I hear a light cough and it is only then that I realise I am not alone.

There is someone in the chair.

I walk over to the window and turn to face the person in the chair. I am surprised by how small the person is. The chair seems to swallow them up, reducing them to the size of a pillow.

The person is female.

Her head rests awkwardly to the right, nestled into the large wing, which makes her look even smaller. Her mouth is open, her eyes closed. I am pleased that she is asleep; it allows me a little more time to process my view. I stare closely at her, just to make sure she is Gramma. Her skin hangs from her cheekbones, as if she is slowly melting. The lines gathered around her mouth suggest she has smiled far less than she has frowned. Along her top lip, pushing through numerous dark hairs, are deep lines which look almost embroidered.

The skin on her neck hangs loose, gathering where her breasts used to be like a paper fan, before disappearing beneath her cream-coloured nightdress. She wears a maroon cardigan, the bottom three buttons fastened around where her waist used to be. On her legs she wears thick black tights, and her feet are posted neatly into tan, sheepskin-lined moccasins. Despite her now being little more than a skeleton, I doubt her ankles would be able to hold her weight.

I stand and stare, conscious that it feels sinister to be doing so. I feel like a voyeur watching the victim of Death's next call.

Her body is slumped to one side and reminds me of a small pile of sandbags.

Or an emptied bag of rags dumped by the roadside.

Chapter 9

My phone vibrates again.

I take it from my pocket and check who the caller is. Surprise, surprise, it's Dad. I quickly switch it off worried that even the vibration may wake Gramma. I push it back in my pocket.

The radiator beneath the window is hot and I stand by it, warming myself, whilst trying to remember Gramma the last time I saw her. It is difficult to draw memories from such a long time ago, especially when you have spent twenty years creating a picture to vilify.

The Gramma I try to remember was far plumper.

She had far fewer visible lines on her face.

She smiled, and when she did, her eyes shone.

Her hair was thick and tidy. Grey, but less so.

The woman in the chair in front of me bears none of these physical traits.

The Gramma I remember tried to please.

She was hard, but she was fair. Her tongue could deliver caustic wit with the speed of a whip.

And, as we found out, she was viciously loyal.

I'm yet to hear her speak, but the woman in the chair in front of me is nothing but a ghost of the Gramma I remember.

My legs are beginning to tire and I check my watch. I've been here forty minutes. I consider whether this is long enough. My dad told me that she didn't have long left. How long is not long? I remember when Sara and I lived together and she was upstairs getting ready, she would shout down to me "I'll not be long..." and that used to mean anything between ten and twenty minutes. In terms of Gramma, it obviously means more than ten minutes (on the basis that I've already been here forty), but how long is not long in rest-of-life terms?

I decide that I'll stay for another twenty minutes to round it up to a full hour. An hour seems a reasonable enough time to remove any residuary traces of guilt. It's not as if she knows I'm here anyway. I'm getting hot, so I remove my rain jacket and fold it neatly on her chest of drawers.

It is clear by the lack of seating that few visitors come here. I am about to sit down on the floor when she coughs again and her eyes flicker slightly. I am instantly excited, as if I am watching a loved one come out of a coma. I feel I should ring a bell or pull the red cord or press the red bleeper or whatever you are supposed to do in these places in an emergency.

Then I realise that this is not an emergency. This is close to the end. These could be her last breaths.

I watch her closely, watch her eyes close again. I decide to stand for the rest of my visit, and I have to admit that I watch the last six minutes pass by on the yellowed plastic clock on the wall above her. I leave it one extra minute and then push myself quietly away from the radiator and take one final look, before making my way past her.

As I reach the back of her chair, she coughs again. I stop dead.

And I wait.

A few moments pass and I hear a grating sound, like she is squeezing air through the narrowest of tubes. She coughs again, and I go back around the chair to see if she is okay.

I watch her lips as they move slowly in a figure of eight movement, rubbing against one another like obese thighs. White saliva joins her lips. It is thick and strong and reminds me of children's glue. She pushes more air out, and then I realise that she is trying to speak. The noises she makes sound ragged, as if loose flaps of skin are vibrating within her throat. I notice a small plastic tumbler of water on the table next to her and place the hard teat against her lips. She sucks on it, and then pushes it away with her tongue. Water drips down her chin, and I take a tissue from a box on the same table and wipe her. Throughout, she keeps her eyes closed. Her lips slow.

I watch her for a few moments longer to ensure she is alright. Then, as I am about to leave for the second time, her mouth opens again and in a croaky voice she forces my name between her gums.

"Samuel."

I am shocked. I don't know how she knew that I was there. I stare at her eyes, trying, and failing, to convince myself that the skin on her eyelids is now so thin she can see through them. Or maybe it's my scent. They say people have their own smell. Maybe she has remembered mine.

"Gramma," I reply softly. The warmth I use when expressing her name surprises me.

Her mouth closes tightly and her eyes flicker, then settle.

I want to take her hand and let her know I am there, but I don't believe for a second that she deserves this kind of treatment from me. Not after the words that left her mouth when Mum vanished. Those types of words are not easily forgotten. Words like that remain part of you, like ink under the skin.

I sink down to the floor and wrap my arms around my knees.

And then I just watch her.

As she silently treads the line between sleep and death.

I end up staying three times longer than I intended.

Chapter 10

The sun is beginning its descent behind the curve of the earth as I take the final fork on my approach home. I haven't taken a direct route, instead preferring to walk through the park and alongside the wider-than-a-stream-but-not-big-enough-to-be-a-river that separates the two pathways.

The park holds so many memories for me and at first it feels strange to be back here. The place where Mum and Tom and I would come and walk endlessly to escape the weight of the air in the house. When Mum sensed that the atmosphere was building to dangerous levels, we would come here, desperate to avoid the poison from my father's mouth, which would spill into every corner of the house like the contents of an overheated pan.

Mum would dash quickly around the house, collecting what she needed, before scooping us up and zipping our coats over whatever we were wearing at the time. Our feet were posted, usually sockless, into wellies and we were off. I have been to this park in pyjamas probably more times than I have fully clothed. But then, whether we were in clothes or not, the only thing on my mum's mind was to get us out of that place as soon as she could. Call it intuition. Call it fight or flight. Judging by the marks that would sometimes be visible on her face, it seemed flight was always the best option. She didn't really stand a chance.

And then, once we were a safe distance away and I heard her breathing slow, she would take us through the park gates and return to being the mother she always was when it was just the three of us.

We would hold hands and jump and sing and splash at the edges of the not-stream-not-river where it was safe. From time to time she would crouch down to our height and teach us the different types of trees; point out different birds and woodland creatures. And then, when we began to tire, she would take us to a bench cut crudely from the trunk of a fallen tree. She would lift us both up so we could sit, and as we struggled to catch our breath she'd reach inside her pockets and find some kind of boiled sweet and maybe a carton of juice.

As we sat and sucked the flavour from the sweet, she would tell us stories of the magical elves and pixies and fairies that came out to dance and play and sing each evening when night had fallen. The woodland creatures would join them for grand balls and banquets at long tables. They would drink from the empty acorn shells that the squirrels had discarded. There was food aplenty, and everyone shared. Everyone smiled. Everyone took care of one another. It sounded like such a happy place, and I was mesmerised.

In hindsight, I think Mum was too. It was clear she was escaping into the world which may or may not have existed when the park closed. Whatever the weather, we would sit on the bench, each knowing that the cold and rain were much less of a worry than what may have lain in store for Mum if we were home.

I reach the bench and I am surprised at how low it now looks. As a child, it seemed like an impossible climb. I sit with my hands in my pockets, my feet outstretched, and watch the water rush by, swollen by the morning rain. From time to time, I am greeted by inquisitive dogs who sniff at my jeans and look longingly for human contact. For love. The sniffs are invariably followed by apologies and the ever sharper pronunciations of the dog's name from somewhere further down the path. I stroke each and every one, my hands getting muddy from doing so. Every creature needs love.

As I consider just how much I would give for a boiled sweet right now, I am greeted like an old friend by a bearded collie who I deduce would usually be grey and white. I'm not sure exactly where he arrives from, but it has to be from somewhere between the trees, as my eyes have been focused on the empty path. He is instantly up on the bench and stretched out on his belly. Then he lays his head on my left thigh and stares up at me through his mud-matted fringe, his deep chocolate eyes asking me something, though I can't work out what it is.

I stroke his coarse hair, from his forehead to the back of his neck. His tail instantly awakens and begins to wag quickly from side to side like a pinball flipper. It hits the damp wood with a dull thud, the sound of joy.

From out of sight, I hear a high-pitched voice which reminds me of an angry witch. "Digby," it shouts sharply, "Digby, come here."

I presume that Digby is the dog lying on me right now. My assumption is based on the flicker of recognition I am sure I saw in his eyes when his name was called. The park is quiet aside from the constant gossiping of the birds and the sound of squirrels above me making their way from branch to branch on seemingly endless acorn-driven parkour runs.

"Diiiiig-beeee. Diiig-beeeee," the witch calls. She is getting closer.

Again, the dog reacts, and I wonder whether it is simply the sound that alerts him, rather than his own name. He pushes out air through his nose, which if he were human would have sounded very much like a sigh.

"Digby!" she says in the tone of a parent trying to shock a toddler into behaving. "Where are you?"

I am watching the path as she comes into view. She is an extremely colourful witch. She wears a purple woollen hat pulled down to just above her eyeline. A long coral-coloured coat stretches from beneath her chin to beneath her knees. It is fastened by a zip which travels diagonally across her chest and could be mistaken for a sleeping bag. The outfit is completed by multi-coloured tie-dye-style wellies.

"Diiiig-beeee! Diiiig-beeee!"

I hold up my hand and wait until she sees me. Then I point at the dog beside me. The woman looks confused at first but quickens her pace. As she gets closer I notice her coat is caked in a similar amount of mud as Digby's.

"Ah, Digby," she says as she gets closer. There is relief in her voice.

I smile at her and notice that this woman couldn't look any less like a witch. It's interesting how a voice and its owner can be so different. The woman's face is round, pudgy and red. I can't work out if the colour is usual or is a palette mixed from her being out of breath from shouting and marching through the woods. She pushes out a deep breath and smiles back.

"I'm so sorry," she says, coming close enough to pat Digby firmly on his side. He sounds hollow.

"It's fine," I say, "don't worry."

I stroke Digby as if to show her that I really don't mind. For a moment we are both touching him.

"I'm getting too old for this," she says.

I'm not sure whether to agree or not, so instead I smile again.

"Do you have a dog?" she asks.

I shake my head and wonder why not. I could do with the company. Then her eyes narrow slightly and I see the same flicker that I saw in Digby's.

"Do you want one?" she asks.

I shake my head and laugh. "Er, no, thanks," I say, again wondering why.

Then, from nowhere, she says, "You're one of the Darte boys, aren't you?"

I'm instantly alert.

"You are, aren't you?" she says, without waiting for an answer. "Terrible business that. How are you?"

I'm not sure whether I should answer her question. I've had years of answering questions on this subject. I've been misquoted and taken out of context more times than I care to remember. I've been tricked and led down paths I would never have travelled without being guided by someone who was only interested in selling more 'news'. That and personal gain. Of course. After all, doesn't that drive most people?

"Oh, y'know," I say, knowing for a fact that she couldn't possibly. I am fairly convinced that the woman is only being polite and isn't some hack in disguise. I am also fairly content that Digby isn't wearing a wire. Even so, my past has taught me to be guarded with my responses.

I am surprised when she says, "I don't. I couldn't possibly. Over the years, though, I've thought about you a lot. You and your brother."

"Thank you," I say. I have to swallow after forcing the final word out.

"Terrible business," she repeats, wiping a clear drip that is about to fall from beneath her nose. I wonder for a second if she is about to cry.

"Are you still at the same house?" she says. "Up on Muddy Lane?"

I tell her I am.

Digby stands suddenly and shakes his head wildly from side to side. The woman and I lift our arms in unison to deflect the compound of mud, tiny sticks, dead leaves and grass which is catapulted through the air towards us.

We wait a few moments until the friendly fire is over. Then we lower our hands and laugh.

"Looks like Digby was after some attention," I say.

"Yes," she says and then continues wistfully, "more than I can give him nowadays."

She attaches Digby's lead and he hops down from the bench and stands dutifully by her side.

"Do you live there alone?" she asks.

"Sorry?"

"At the house. Do you live there alone?"

For the second time, I am surprised by her question. Drawing the response hurts. In my chest. In my heart.

"I do now," I say.

She nods to herself, as if confirming something silently.

"Well," she says, "I'd better get on my way. He's going to need a bath."

"Rather you than me," I say, smiling.

She smiles back, her eyes seemingly investigating what is behind mine.

Chapter 11

The mud has started to dry by the time I begin peeling my clothes off in the kitchen. I push them into the washing machine and make my way upstairs in just my boxer shorts. As usual the doors on the landing are closed, apart from my room at the back and the bathroom. I realise that it makes the whole landing much darker and perhaps a little more sinister than it needs to be; however, it just feels better this way. An open door will only provide me with more questions. Another room in which to sit and consider the past.

I shower and dry and pull on a t-shirt and pyjama bottoms. I am about to leave my bedroom when my phone rings. I know who it is before I even pick it up from the duvet.

Someone – I forget who – once told me that I could set up different ringtones for different people, so that there would be no surprises when the phone burst into action. For a short while I followed their advice, assigning different tones to different contacts. It didn't work for me, though. I found that I preferred there to be at least a small possibility that my intuition was wrong when the phone rang.

I spin the phone to find I am correct.

"Hello?" I say, purposefully giving the impression that I am surprised by the caller's identity. After all these years I still forget that my first greeting will be the recorded message before my father comes on the phone. I chuckle to myself, vowing to answer, "What the fuck do you want?" next time my dad's name flashes up on the phone.

And then, after the message that tells me where he is calling from – I hear his voice.

"Sam?"

"Aha," I say, trying to sound casual.

"What are you laughing at?"

"Nothing," I say, unaware that the call had connected before I heard his voice.

"You with someone?" he says bluntly.

"No. I'm alone."

"Did you go and see her?"

A part of me wants to lie and answer that I didn't. If I tell him the truth then it gives the impression that he still has an element of control over me. Some kind of hold, which even after all of these years he can implement to get his own way. It has taken me many years to release myself from his grip and make decisions for myself. It hasn't been easy. Now, I reach inside my mind for the lessons I've learned in my therapy sessions. For the sake of my own sanity, I have to make it clear that anything I do is not down to his say-so. That his grip has gone. Subconsciously, I question whether there is any truth in this statement.

"No," I say unconvincingly.

"You did," he snaps back. "You went this morning."

"So why ask?" I say.

"Wanted to know if you'd lie. How was she?"

I ignore his attempt to take control. "She's dying, Dad."

"I know that. Did you speak?"

"No. She slept."

"Are you going again?"

"I've not thought about it," I lie. I spent a good part of the afternoon wandering in the park and thinking about it.

"Samuel," he says, the use of my full name a well-worn (and transparent) tactic.

I say nothing. For once, it is quiet where he is. There is no background noise, none of the usual sounds which envelop our calls. Male voices shouting, arguing. Laughter. The occasional sound of frustration – a telephone handset being repeatedly returned to its cradle at high speed.

Today, I can hear him breathing.

"Sam? Sam?" I hear a little desperation in his voice. "You still there?"

I pause for as long as I feel I can, then I simply say, "Yes." I am pleased at how strong it sounds.

"Listen. I want you to go again," he says.

And then he hangs up the phone.

After an hour of watching the news repeated on the television, I try to plan my evening ahead. I vowed to give up watching the news, on the basis that I have become cynical and distrustful of pretty much everything I read or hear. It is almost second nature to me now to hear a news story, instantly disregard it and look for the real reason why the broadcasters have chosen to share this information. The news is the whipped cream spread over the top of the trifle. The real reason it has been broadcast – its real agenda – lays in the jelly and fruit and sponge beneath.

It has become a trait of mine to look for a hidden agenda. As would anyone who has been in my position.

I used to hate people who thought like this. I used to watch them on television sharing their conspiracy theories with the world and essentially being made to look foolish by raised eyebrows and smirks from the television presenters. Ultimately, the gargantuan broadcasting corporations crush those smaller groups who are searching for the truth. The corporations decide whether a story gathers momentum, and usually when people are coming too close to the truth, they are ridiculed and tossed to one side by world governments colluding with the media to ensure traction is lost.

The strategy is to show the 'crazy' people on our screens from time to time (the people who have had alien encounters or have proof as to why a government may kill its own elected leader) simply to debunk their theories. To isolate these people. To make sure that those watching feel so disconnected from them that they become laughing stocks. And whatever truth they are claiming is crushed like ice in a blender.

I am still drawn to the news. I hope that my mum's face will one day return to the country's screens. The picture of her smiling at the picnic. The one where the position of the sun makes it impossible to see the lack of light behind her eyes. I glance at the frame on the coffee table and smile, then swallow.

I decide to order food, and it takes me half an hour to conclude that my wallet is not in the house. I know where it is. It's in the pocket of my rain jacket. And that pocket, along with the rest of the jacket, is folded neatly on the chest of drawers a few feet away from where my gramma sleeps.

I resolve to return to St Dymphna's in the morning to collect it.

I begin to flick through television channels, wondering whether Gramma will still be breathing by the time I arrive.

I am hopeful this whole charade will be over by then.

Chapter 12

I wake, shower and I am in my office (the room formerly known as the dining room) twenty minutes before my first meeting begins, at eight. The sky outside is dark again, and huge grey clouds billow across my eyeline at high speed. The clouds are set against a blood-red background, as the sun desperately tries to make itself known.

I log in to my work server and watch as, one by one, the colleagues I have never met follow suit. Soon, I am told that we have reached the quorum for the 'meeting' to begin. So begins three hours of 'discussion' over how we tackle a new project the company is pitching for.

The system works well, allowing each member of the meeting to type or speak their responses to various technical questions posed about mainframes, servers and a whole host of other specialisms. I am an unnecessary participant in today's meeting; I could have opted out. When given the chance, though, I usually opt in for these meetings. This way it appears I am always willing and always working.

As the vast majority of staff work from home, we are told that we must log in and work for a specific number of hours each week. Meetings are a great way of achieving these hours, especially meetings where your presence is unnecessary and you can sit invisibly daydreaming or surfing the net or reading. It stretches the definition of the word 'work' almost to snapping point. To amuse myself, I pull the dictionary from the line of books stacked neatly on the shelves next to my desk and open it.

work /wəːk/ *noun*
an activity, such as a job, that a person uses physical or mental effort to do, usually for money

I laugh to myself, pleased that I am correct in thinking that a good proportion of my day-to-day activities couldn't be further from the dictionary definition.

As the rain begins to fall outside, my eyes are drawn to the top of the garden where my father's vegetable patch used to be. Now all that remains is a large pile of excavated earth that sits alongside an empty hole. I imagine that after all this rain, the hole will be partially filled with water again.

Many years after my mum vanished, my father applied to have her be legally treated as dead. He told me and Tom that the reason for this was so he could move on with his life. It seemed that he wanted everything that reminded him of Mum neatly packed away in a box, never to be opened again.

Later, after what happened to Dad, it turned out that Mum being 'dead' did have some other benefits aside from simply setting his mind at rest. And in time, it turned out that those benefits legally transferred to Tom and me. And so I ended up with the family home and a couple more zeroes on the end of my bank balance than I had ever seen before. And Tom...well, he received even more zeroes, which would ultimately make their way up his nose night after night after endless night.

One day, soon after the house became mine, I went up into the loft and found that neatly packed box and opened it. That was where I found the picture of Mum at the picnic. That, and a number of other secrets.

Secrets that would teach me that you should always remove the mask and look beneath before making a judgement about anything.

Chapter 13

Ting.

The meeting comes to a close with a pleasing chiming sound. There follows a flurry of ringing noises, not unlike how I imagine a machine gun firing handbells would sound. We are all in such a rush to leave the meeting that if this was twenty years ago there would be a huge crush – a bottleneck – at the door.

I return to my home screen, which the company playfully calls MySnug. It shows just how out of touch they are with my generation's tendency to sneer at anything that seems like a blatant attempt to control us. Or maybe that's just me.

The top right of my screen shows the numbers

2.54
-32.06

The top number shows how many hours I have worked this week and the second how many hours to go. My company is flexible, so you can pretty much work when you want. Don't get me wrong, I don't just sit silently in meetings every day. No, I have allotted projects to do. But I have been with the company long enough to know that none of the projects ever get finished due to either a change in management, a lack of funding or the dissolution of a government project. Therefore, we are pursuing projects and undertaking work that we already know will not become what they were established to be. Sure, some of our code may end up bastardised in some other project in the future, but never the project we set out to finish. Therefore, armed with this knowledge, I've realised that it doesn't matter whether I ever finish my given work.

I don't want to give the wrong impression, some days I could cry, I'm so laden with the yearning for some kind of meaningful work.

But I've had too much else to do.

Too much to process; too much to understand.

And a job of this nature has allowed me to concentrate on those things.

Allowed me to make this journey.

The single peal of the church bell tells me that it's one o'clock by the time I reach St Dymphna's. The sky above me begins to growl. The air is unusually warm, the trees heavy with day after day of torrential water.

I reach the door and am almost instantly greeted by Tony, who (rather inappropriately) instructs me to "Come".

He spins and I follow him down the corridor. I notice the same door is open and I glance in as we pass. It takes me a moment to realise that the only difference from yesterday is that today the bed is neatly made and empty. I sign in, and he takes me down the corridor toward Gramma.

"Terrible night," he says. "Te-rib-ull." He wipes his eyes with his sleeve. "Sorry," he sniffles.

I ask him what happened, and he tells me that they lost two residents in the night, including, it turns out, the one from the front corridor. He looks tired. Both mentally and physically exhausted.

"I'm sorry," I say, considering for a moment how I would feel if my job reduced me to tears.

"It's okay. It's okay. Part of the job."

I smile.

"Don't get 'ny easier, though," he says.

We get to Gramma's room and he disappears inside. A moment later, he reappears and beckons me in.

We pass just as I get inside the door. "She's awake," he says. I take this as some kind of warning, and then he is gone. The door clicks shut behind me, and I am surprised to see that Gramma's chair has been moved and is no longer facing the window. Instead, it has been turned ninety degrees and now faces the foot of her bed.

She is sitting in the same position in the chair, her head resting on the wing to the right. But unlike yesterday, her eyes are open and they follow me until I am standing awkwardly in front of her.

"Won't you sit?" she croaks. It seems a strain to push the words out.

She watches as I look around me and then interrupts sharply: "On the bed, Samuel."

I sit, and we are directly opposite one another, a matter of feet separating our feet. She is dressed in the same clothing as yesterday and I pick up an unfamiliar scent from her. It reminds me of straw and soil and unwashed clothes that have been left beneath a bed or in the bottom of a wardrobe for months.

I see for the first time that her eyes have a glassy look. The blueish-grey eyes are hidden behind a transparent, thick-looking liquid. It causes a constant weeping from her tear ducts and leaves a shiny residue in the corner of her eyes. I offer her a tissue and she refuses with a slight shake of her head. I decide that it is simply because she has her eyes open that she looks less dead, less skeletal. It is clear that she cannot have changed physically during the last twelve hours.

"How are you?" I say.

"I had breakfast," she says, weakly lifting a crooked finger in the direction of the table alongside her. A few remaining cornflakes float on the surface of the slightly oranged milk. The spoon provides a potential means of escape to dry land for them. Alongside the bowl is her tip-cup, which is half-filled with what looks like tea. Condensation drips from the inside of the teat.

I am not sure what to say. I am here for my jacket and my wallet. I am not here to make conversation with this woman. Indeed, I don't know where to start after, well...everything.

"Oh," I manage.

"Cereal," she croaks. It sounds like her words are being pushed through the tightest of gaps.

"Nice?" I ask.

"It's cereal, Samuel" – she takes a deep breath – "don't tell me you've not tried it."

For the second time in the last few moments, I am unsure. Was there something pointed in what she said? Was it some kind of dig from times past? The only thing I am sure of is that her tone sounds like my father's. Direct and to the point. No fucking around.

"I have, yes. Sorry," I find myself saying.

"Good. Then you'll know."

I glance to my left and notice my jacket isn't where I left it.

"So," she says, lifting her head to face me, "have you come to see me die?"

"Er. No. I've come because –"

"Your father sent you."

Lying isn't an option. After what this woman has done over so many years, I no longer have the ability or desire to make her feel any better. So I tell the truth.

"Correct. He asked me to come."

"To watch me die?"

"I suppose."

She raises the thin, almost invisible hairs where her eyebrows once were. I believe I see a glimpse of understanding in the wetness of her eyes, though this could be wishful thinking on my part. A new drip forms in the corner of each eye. Suddenly, she begins to cough and I can hear the sound of sticky fluid and phlegm being brought up from her lungs and then deposited again. It crackles in her throat and chest.

I watch for a moment as her tear ducts begin to fill and overflow. Liquid runs down her cheeks. Still she tries to catch her cough, either to force out the blockage or resign it back to her lungs. Her forehead furrows and she points with a limp hand toward herself. It is clear I have to act.

I am up in less than a second and reaching across her to grab the tip-cup from the table. I sip it to ensure that it isn't too hot and my mouth is filled with lukewarm milky tea. Whoever made it hasn't gone easy on the sugar. Then I get on my knees alongside her, holding the cup to her mouth. She takes small mouthfuls, coughing between each. Droplets of tea land mainly on my hand, a few on my face.

We repeat this until she coughs loudly and a piece of phlegm the size of a coin leaves her mouth and lands on my shoulder. I see blood mixed in with the lime-coloured stringy puddle. Then she takes a further sip and her coughing subsides. She is finally able to breathe again.

I take a tissue and wipe the residue of spit and tea from around her mouth. Then I take another and dab both of her eyes. The skin around her eyes is translucent and I can see a mysterious tangle of cerulean capillaries running off in all directions.

Her scent is far stronger from here and seems to be coming from her cardigan. She smells stale, like she has already died. The urge to retch is difficult to contain and I have to pull away from her. I take another tissue from the box and wipe my hands and face. Then I scoop the phlegm from my jumper and screw the tissue into a tight ball and place it on the table.

I sit back on the bed.

"I'm tired," she says.

"Okay. Are you sure you're alright?"

She smiles weakly. "Yes. Never better."

Without thinking, I smile at her use of irony.

Her eyes flicker, and she rests her head on the wing again.

"Er, I left my jacket yesterday. Have you seen it?" I ask, certain that she'll be asleep any second.

Her eyes are closed.

I watch her for a few moments. Enjoying her peace.

She is asleep.

I collect the dirty tissues from the table and drop them in the bin as I leave the room.

Chapter 14

I pop my head into the office as I leave the home.

Tony appears to be playing some kind of online card game. Poker, I think. He jumps slightly when he realises that I am at the doorframe and then rotates his body in a vain attempt to cover the screen.

"Can I 'elp?" he says, quickly reapplying his smile.

"I hope so. I left my jacket in my gramma's room yesterday and it seems to have been moved?"

"Okay," he says matter-of-factly.

There is a brief pause and I sense he wants me to say something else.

"I just wondered if you'd seen it?"

"No. Not me. No, no, sorry."

"Could the cleaners maybe have moved it?"

"Ah, yes, maybe," he says. "Could be in lost property." He motions to a small cupboard in the corner of the room. "It's locked. We keep it safe."

"Okay, great," I say. "Can we check?"

"I have no key. My manager, she comes to work tonight."

"Right."

"You call her. Susan. Call Susan. She can tell you about the jacket, yes?"

"Okay, what time?"

"Susan come at six. She will help."

I check my watch. Six is only four hours away. "Okay, six?" I confirm.

"Yes, yes," Tony says, and then he stands, which I believe is a prompt for me to leave.

He looks flustered as he approaches me, like some unknown incident has occurred that he must deal with urgently. I can feel his eyes on my back as I reach the external door, so I turn to check.

He is watching me.

"Oh, Tony," I say, having almost forgotten, "how is she, generally?"

"Mrs Joan?"

I nod.

"Mrs Joan not good. Not long for her now. I'm sorry."

I pull a smile as if to thank him and press the door release button to leave.

Chapter 15

I return home, my thoughts swimming like fish in an aquarium.

I log back in to MySnug and busy myself with responding to emails and opening and closing various spreadsheets and documents. I worked out a while ago that one of the performance indicators for employees is how often they work on certain files as part of a project. A digital log shows the last time you opened a file. The system is flawed in its simplicity: it doesn't matter how long you spend on the file, it is simply logged that you 'worked' on it. Therefore, I log in to all my project files on a daily basis so it appears that I am working to move the project along.

For the vast majority of employees, the system probably works, simply because they don't know of its existence. Because none of the employees have ever met face to face, we have built no particular loyalty to one another, so we keep discoveries like this – system workarounds, if you will – to ourselves. Well, almost always. Every now and again, someone comes along with whom you find you have something in common. In general terms, though, it makes sense to keep quiet and keep a competitive advantage.

The sun shines brightly through the doors which separate my office from the conservatory. I check the all-important numbers.

6.06
-28.54

Six hours down. Twenty nine to go. I log off, the final straw being that I cannot be bothered to expend energy in closing all the blinds in the conservatory. I've done enough for one day.

I stand and walk over to the conservatory, standing just to the left of the doors to avoid the direct sunlight.

Soon after my mum disappeared, my dad decided that it was a good idea to make some alterations to our home. He decided that the house needed a conservatory and set about building one. He hired equipment to pull up the old patio, and beneath where it once sat, he built foundations for the near-empty room I am now staring at. He told us at the time that Gramma may come and stay for a while, and he didn't think we would want to share the largest television with her and her programmes. It made perfect sense. He also told me that he needed a project. 'Something to get my teeth into' were his words, I think. The conservatory became his distraction, and after he had finished it, it did go on to be used. At least for a while.

Now, all I see is a room carpeted in navy and vacant apart from four grey beanbags, which sit centrally like a cluster of volcanic islands, and, in the corner, an old television stand that has grown furry with dust. I couldn't tell you what happened to the television. The windowsills that run down three sides of the room are equally dusty, and I feel a tickle in my throat just looking at them.

I am back at St Dymphna's at exactly six o'clock.

I did consider telephoning to ask the manager whether my jacket was there, but something made me feel hopeful and I decided to walk around instead. That way if the jacket is there (which I expect it will be), I can simply collect it.

I ring the bell and wait.

There is no response.

I wait for a few minutes and then push the doorbell again. Instantly, a frowning Tony appears from the office and opens the door. He lets me in silently and begins to lead me toward the visitors' book. I stop him.

"I'm here about my coat," I say, "not to visit."

"Yes, yes, yes," he says in a way that suggests I have spent the entire afternoon shadowing him and repeatedly asking about the coat. "Sit, please. I go see."

I sit on one of the two chairs which sandwich the table where the visitors' book lies. Strangely, the chairs don't look like chairs to sit on. They are wooden and covered in a garish gold-and-yellow-striped fabric. Golden tassels hang from anywhere that will have them. They look like something that the genie from Aladdin would have in his house. Or Elton John. I notice that all the doors that line the corridor are closed. I also notice, for the first time, several low-quality pictures of (what I imagine are) staff with their arms around (what I imagine are) now-deceased residents. The staff in the photographs smile widely, the residents less so. I spot Tony in a number of pictures. He looks much younger with hair.

Just then the office door reopens and I leap up, still unsure whether the chairs are to be used for their original purpose. Tony appears. In his hand is my coat. He holds it up and smiles broadly. He reminds me of a wild game hunter.

"Your coat?" he says, pushing it into my arms.

"Thank you," I say, squeezing the pocket to ensure my wallet is there. It is.

"Good, good, good," he says hurriedly, "I must go."

And he does.

Ten minutes later, I am, unexpectedly, sitting on the edge of Gramma's bed. She is surprised to see me, just as I am surprised to be here. I notice that a little colour has entered her cheeks.

"Hello, again," she says, her voice dry and raspy.

"Do you need a drink or something?" I ask.

She shakes her head, then reconsiders "maybe a gin?"

I smile.

"And some peanuts."

"How have you been?"

"Dying," she says with a slight smile. "I've been dying since you left."

I return her smile and shake my head slightly.

"Are you staying?" she asks, noticing that I am wearing my rain jacket.

"No," I reply, "there was just something I needed to do."

She stares at me.

I stand and open the wardrobe. I take various hangers from the rail and hold up a number of cardigans for her. She seems happy to see some of these items again and chooses quickly. A few minutes later, I have peeled the maroon cardigan from her and replaced it with the tan one she chose. She uses a bony hand to finger the pearl sequins which run in swirls down the front. She seems content.

"Thank you, Samuel," she says.

I take a step back. "That's better," I say.

"Are you leaving?" she asks.

"Yes, I have to go now."

"Could I have a little perfume?" she asks, pointing toward the chest of drawers.

"Sure."

I find the perfume immediately, remove the lid and pass it to her. She shakily pours a small amount onto her fingers and then dabs it on her neck and wrists. She passes the bottle back to me. I replace the lid and return it to the drawer.

"Will you come again?" she asks.

I panic at the question and feel I have no choice but to reply in the affirmative. At that moment, her eyes begin to run, and she slowly dabs them with a balled-up tissue that has more creases than her skin. She posts the tissue into her cardigan sleeve.

"When?" she says.

"Er..."

"Did I mention I'm dying?" she says, and I am sure she attempts a wink.

"Soon," I reply.

"Well, don't leave it too long."

"I won't."

I close the door behind me, and I am instantly hit by the smell from the cardigan. Stupidly, I sniff at my hand and feel the bile rise in my stomach. I just make it to the toilet before the vomit comes from my throat and down my nose.

I put the cardigan in a swing-top bin and begin scrubbing my hands.

Chapter 16

A helicopter flies above as I fumble for my key and push open the front door.

My phone rings as I slip my trainers off in the hall. I already know who it is. I pull the phone from my pocket and shut the call down. I can't deal with my dad today. There are so many reasons that I am angry with him, and the most recent one is the fact that the burden of Gramma has been passed to me. I would be well within my rights to refuse to go and see her – or to apply pressure to Tom – but I realise that the energy needed to harangue Tom will likely outweigh the effort it takes to visit. After all, as Dad and Tony pointed out, she hasn't got long left.

I hang my jacket on the newel and make my way into the office. My first thought is to log on and do a couple more hours' work, but as soon as I see my mum's photograph, my attention is diverted. I turn and move toward the door, as if guided.

Ten minutes later, I am back in the office, the heating on, accompanied by a brown storage box. I remove the packaging tape from the edges, which tears off the cutaway handle. Then I lift the lid and take out the huge pile of papers.

I have been through this box before, many times, hoping for some kind of clue as to what happened to my mum. I am not entirely sure where the information in the box originally came from. Some papers appear to be in my dad's handwriting – his own investigation (if you like). The majority are police reports of phone calls, witness statements and that type of thing. And then there are photographs and some notes beautifully written in script, each one dated and annotated with my gramma's name.

I don't know what I am looking for, but the realisation hits me that when Gramma dies, her knowledge will be lost. It will be silently taken with her six feet beneath the ground and left to rot. Alternatively, all she knows about my mum's disappearance will be incinerated at eight hundred degrees and probably passed to me in an urn. And with that, it is likely that any chance of a resolution will be lost forever. My life will be left in a confused spiral. Reduced to nothing but a sewing box full of tangled threads.

I am not sure that I can continue this way.

All that my mum left behind on the day she walked out on us was her wedding ring, her engagement ring and a note. Oh, and Dad.

And me.

And Tom.

And any hope of a normal life for any of us.

On that morning, Tom and I stood on the empty drive in the bright sunshine for well over half an hour. Just staring. I suggested that we sit down, and we probably lost a further hour sitting in silence, lifting our heads expectantly each time we heard the engine of a car.

Eventually (as we were wondering whether Dad had left too), there was a large cough and a snapping noise and my dad's beige Volkswagen Passat estate rolled around the corner. We watched as he made his way up the steep drive and we heard the click-click-click of the handbrake as it was stretched to its maximum. We were both at the car door before my dad had a chance to open it. Tom had already begun to cry. As Dad climbed from the car, I asked him as calmly as I could about the note and whether he had seen Mum.

He told me that he had been up early that morning, loading the car with garden waste – branches, black sacks, that type of thing. He wanted to get to the tip before it got busy. He had left Mum in bed, fast asleep. I tried to pull him toward the house, but I wasn't strong enough. He shook off my grip easily. He didn't seem to be in any hurry to see the note. Instead, he was going to clean out the boot of his car.

He shouted at Tom to stop crying, and I managed to hold back my own emotions so as not to annoy him any further. It physically hurt the inside of my throat to do so.

"She'll be back," he said.

It wasn't until eight days later that he reported her missing. Each time Tom or I asked, he used those same three words, until I think he had stopped believing them himself. By then he had already dug the foundations for the conservatory.

I begin to sort through the pile of papers, which I've fanned out across the floor. I have an instant déjà vu feeling, aware that I have sorted these papers on numerous occasions before. Nevertheless, I am still convinced that I can find the answer to what really happened. A conviction that lies somewhere between this box and my gramma, a mile or so away.

I decide to put the papers into chronological order so I can piece together the exact events in the order they occurred.

I have to be careful not to take anything as the truth.

This box has always, somehow, been empty of truth.

Real truth.

Chapter 17

I am awake very early; the sky is still black. My sleep has been punctuated by dreams and fantasies of my mum returning, leaving, taking off her rings, returning again, hugging me, singing, leaving, returning. I feel happy that I have survived the cruelness that the darkness often brings. That is why my lamp stays on twenty-four hours a day. Just in case.

My thoughts turn instantly to the box which sits, fractured and empty, in the room below me. I have had this feeling before, an inspiration from somewhere far beyond my understanding that somehow I can solve the mystery. The reengagement with Gramma has surely ignited something within.

My mind then turns to work.

And then instantly to Gramma.

After my mum went missing, my dad was unable to cope with a full-time job and looking after two young boys. On top of this, he was also dealing with the police, who arrived most days to speak to him. It would usually be the same two fellas who came, neither dressed in uniform. Without their knowledge, Tom and I nicknamed them Red-Face and Tall. All you need to know is that one was tall and thin, like an early-twentieth-century headmaster. The other was smaller, chubbier and red-faced. Some of their visits were short. Others went on for hours, and my neck would ache from straining to hear what was going on behind the lounge door.

From time to time my dad would insist the policemen left. I would hear his voice getting louder, his anger bubbling to the surface like hot pasta. It was only when he lost his temper that I managed to hear anything that went on behind that closed door. And then it would only be his voice that I heard. The rest of the time the constant stream of discussion was nothing more than a low, muffled drone. The dull hum of a distant motorway.

Occasionally, the police would arrive in numbers, and once or twice they erected a white tent in the back garden to work beneath. Each time they left with a look of disappointment on their faces. Our garden or vegetable patch would be four feet lower, with a huge termites' nest of mud alongside it. They never did tidy it up. That fell on Dad. And sometimes me.

I work for four hours and finally see the winter sun pricking a pin hole of light in the desolate and terminally grey sky.

10.06
-24.54

I'm tired, but pleased that I have managed to get so much work shifted even before the sun started its day. I have no meetings until this afternoon, which leaves me pretty much free for a good proportion of the day. I log off, then leave my chair and get back to the papers on the floor.

I make a coffee and spend a few hours continuing to sort the papers into order. I find a date on each document and place it into a pile based on the year that it happened. I am trying not to read any of the documents; it seems a better idea to get everything in order before studying them in any detail. There are two reasons for this.

The first is that I want to start from the very beginning again. By doing so, perhaps I can retrace my own life and that of my brother. Maybe it will help me with my recollections of the past. It's a long shot but I hope that Gramma will be able to verify at least some of my memories and perhaps help me lay the mystery to rest. Or incinerate it.

The second reason is that I have already read these papers over and over again in the past. In fact, somewhere among the papers will be the notes I made when I last did so. I know from experience that I can easily get lost down rabbit holes of some enormity by following witness statements and interviews. The first rule is to keep in mind that every single recorded piece of evidence may or may not be true. Of course, some of the statements will be the truth. Others will be words deftly massaged by the police to make sure that the 'correct' evidence fits. This enables them to disregard the information that doesn't. Some will be outright lies. Don't get me wrong, I'm not hopeful that I will find anything new or pertinent by retracing my steps again. But I am determined to give it one last try.

My neck is beginning to stiffen, so I pull myself across the floor and lean my back against the foot of an armchair. I let out a large sigh and massage my neck and shoulders with my hands. I can feel small pockets in my muscles popping as I knead them. I don't know whether this is normal, but it feels good.

After a few minutes, I reach over and collect an assortment of photographs which seem desperate to force their way out of the sides of the battered thick manila envelope that they are housed in. My heart begins to pump faster and I'm not sure why. I have seen these photographs tens of times before. I have nothing to fear.

As my mum vanished without a trace, there are, of course, no crime scene photographs. Or perhaps I should say, no crime scene photographs which depict my mum covered in blood, or with strangle marks around her neck, or her grey hand reaching from some shallow grave in the middle of rural

England. No graphic pictures of her flesh spilling out like bloodied sponge onto the tarmac beside her. There are no pictures of her being brought over the side of a police boat, her body wrapped in bin bags which have finally split, leaking the rocks onto the bottom of the lake and sending my mother to the surface. There is no murder weapon. No crime scene. No body. No nothing.

I leaf through the pictures: some are colour, others black and white. I see pictures of the kitchen table. Pictures of the note. Pictures of my mother's engagement ring. Her wedding ring.

Of all three.

Pictures of the house from the outside.

Pictures of the garden.

Of my parents' bedroom.

Of the dressing table.

Of the wardrobe (doors closed).

Of the wardrobe (doors open).

Of every single garment in there.

Pictures of each and every room. From all angles.

Of the car.

Of the inside of the car.

Of the boot of the car.

Of the shed.

Of the tools hanging there.

The spade.

The hammer.

The axe.

There are at least a hundred photographs of the last three. A few distance shots, but mainly heavily zoomed close-up shots. The handle. The blade. The hammer head. A slight chip in the metal. A maroon discolouration in the grain of the wood. It could be said that based on photographs alone it was pretty clear what the police favoured as their evidence. Something for them to work on.

If you were unclear as to what you were looking at, you could mistake the vast majority of these photographs as belonging to somebody who has decided to sell all their worldly possessions including their house and car. In my opinion, they offer little evidential value. I place them back on the floor on top of the manila envelope, suspecting that it will simply disintegrate if asked to hold on to these photographs any longer.

Outside, lightweight clouds swirl at high speed across a charcoal sky. The sky is ready to open again. I decide to leave for the nursing home before that happens. I pull on my trainers and grab my jacket from the bottom of the stairs. I take out my wallet to store it safely in my jeans pocket. I have a fear that one day I will become stuck somewhere without money.

My therapist and I have explored this fear in some detail and we concluded it probably comes from the uncertainty over my mum's final resting place. That I have somehow conjured up a mental narrative that has Mum, suffering from amnesia, lost and lonely in some isolated place. If only she had taken her purse with her, some money, then maybe she could have found a way to contact us. And come home. Instead, my narrative has her dying in the wilderness, tired, hungry and alone.

It is this thought that drives me to open my wallet to ensure I have some cash. Of course, I haven't. The notes and piles upon piles of receipts stuffed in there are gone. It was the addition of the notes that fattened out my wallet to the size of a large hamburger. Discomfort was the reason that I transferred the wallet to my jacket in the first place. And now it's empty. I estimate that two to three hundred pounds is missing. Oh, and maybe fifty indiscriminate receipts.

I put the wallet into my jeans pocket and zip up my coat, annoyed that I didn't notice the lightness of the wallet the previous evening. It is also frustrating that I now have a further mystery to solve.

It is only when I am halfway to St Dymphna's that I realise I am wearing ripped jeans. And a *Cannibal Corpse* t-shirt. With the lyrics from their single 'Hammer Smashed Face' adorning the back.

Chapter 18

When I arrive, Tony is nowhere to be seen and instead I am greeted by a person I've not met before. Susan.

Susan is small in height and large in both depth and width. Her nurse's uniform is being stretched to its limit in every direction and the dark-blue belt holding down her over-long smock looks ready to snap. Her badge tells me that she is the manager of the home.

She asks who I am here to visit and I tell her. She smiles, and with a slight flick of her pointed tongue, she licks her top lip. I hope that this is just a reflex and has no deeper meaning. On another day, I would have been forgiven for expecting her to unravel her tongue and suck me in like a chameleon. It is clear I look like lunch.

I sign in, and as we reach Gramma's door, I grasp my opportunity and turn to Susan. "I was just wondering, because I left my coat yesterday, who is in charge of looking after lost property?"

"You left your coat?" She looks confused, eyeing the coat that I am wearing.

"Yes, I –"

"Isn't that it?" she says, nodding.

"It is, but –"

Just then a red light appears between her breasts and she lifts her lanyard. "Emergency," she says. "Sorry."

As if not understanding her true girth, she accidentally pushes me into the wall and is gone.

I am surprised to see that Gramma's chair is now half-facing the bed, half the door. It seems to rotate like the hands on a clock each day.

As I enter, she opens her eyes and smiles warmly. I am conflicted but smile back. It seems a little harsh to ignore the smile of a dying woman, despite our past. She looks better than the day before and it seems that she has asked one of the staff members to brush her hair and apply a little powdered colour to each cheek. I think it would have been called rouge back in her day.

I sit on the bed opposite her and she asks me to pour the tea. I notice that her voice is stronger, like her words are no longer being caught by cobwebs in her throat. There are two cups and a steel teapot covered in a striped tea cosy. I am not sure how she knew when I was coming, but steam is still leaving the spout. The tea can't have been there long. I pour us both a cup and place hers on the table alongside her. I quickly realise that her tea should be in her tip-cup instead. I reach over and am about to decant one into the other when she lifts her hand and speaks again.

"I'll manage," she says.

I sip my tea, happy to feel the sugar course through my veins.

In a slow, low voice she says, "So, you came back to see the almost dead one."

"Don't say that, Gramma."

"Well, it's true."

I smile. I know she is trying to put me at ease.

"Why are you here, Samuel?"

There are many answers to this question. And none of them are: through my own choice. I could repeat that my father asked me to come. I could also say I'm here because I owe it to my mum to try to mine for information before the pit permanently closes down. I could even say I'm here because I left my jacket. Instead, I choose the vaguest of options.

"Well," I say, "I suppose there are a number of reasons. But mainly I'm here because I know that you haven't got long left."

"Right you are, dear," she says disbelievingly.

"It's true," I say weakly.

"I've had plenty of time to think about you," she says. "I'm just glad I got to see you again."

"Me too," I say. I think I mean it.

"Not like your father."

"No, it's a shame he can't come to visit, but..." My words trail off. The elephant is far too large for Gramma's small room. I don't want to begin a conversation that I can't finish. I feel like I am in a large crowd of people watching a house burn down and we are all complaining about how warm we are.

"It is a shame," she says and dabs her eye.

The china cup rattles against the saucer as she lifts them both onto her lap. She takes a sip of her tea and replaces the cup. A small amount of tea forms a moat around the base of the cup.

"And Thomas?" she asks.

I tell her about Tom's aim to make his way in the music world and she listens, though I am not sure how much she understands. She tells me that Tom was always a dreamer, but from a young age he wanted everything to be done for him. Though I don't say it, I have to agree. She asks where he is living and rolls her watery eyes when I tell her he is in London.

"I expected Los Angeles," she says. "And will he make it in the pop world?"

"I very much doubt it," I say, conscious that in the last fifteen years I haven't heard him play once; he still hasn't got a band together; and it appears that most days are spent in a hazy kaleidoscope of drink, drugs and God knows what else.

"And what about you, dear?" she says.

"Me?"

She mock looks around the room.

I smile. "What do you want to know?"

"How are you?"

"I'm okay," I say, my eyes wandering somewhere far away.

"I see that you still have that look."

My brow furrows.

"That look, the one that tells me you're trying to understand the world around you."

"Do I?"

I think I already know the answer to this question. It's something that Sara said to me many times. She used to call it my solar system eyes. I understood that to mean that I was not concentrating on my immediate proximity, that I had got lost somewhere in the conversation we were having. At first she thought it was cute that my mind could take me to distant places. That I was a deep thinker, always considering every angle. Near the end, it was 'irritating', and at the very end, it was simply 'plain fucking rude'.

"Yes, dear."

"I suppose I am," I say honestly. "Trying to understand the world, that is."

"You don't change, Samuel."

She sips her tea again, and I do the same, if for no other reason than to not have to fill the silence. I watch as she drinks, and pretend I am still drinking as she shakily returns cup to saucer.

"Are you married?" she says, and before I can respond she continues, "Children?"

"No, no children. I suppose, strictly speaking, I am married. But we're not, y'know, together."

She looks genuinely concerned. "Oh dear. I am sorry."

"It's okay. Really it is."

The door could not have opened at a better time. I wasn't keen on where that conversation was going. Tony takes a few steps into the room.

"Mrs Joan," he says, "it's lunchtime."

"Is it?" she says.

"Yes. You come now?"

"Yes, dear," she says – and instantly I feel deflated.

She then turns to me. "It's a cold lunch, so I won't be long. You will wait for me, won't you?"

Chapter 19

By the time Gramma returns, I am close to sleep on her bed. My feet are on the floor, my head on one of her pillows. It must be a combination of the incredible heat in the room and the time I chose to leave my bed this morning.

The door opening startles me and I sit up quickly. Somewhere in my dreams I was getting closer to the answer. I rub my eyes. Tony helps her from her wheelchair into the high-backed chair, and then he leaves the room and returns with a tray of fresh tea. He places it on the table.

"Ah, it's good you have coat," he says, touching his own collar.

"Er, yeah," I reply.

"That's good, good, good," he says, pouring the tea. He passes me a cup. I am about to ask him about the vacancy in my wallet, but he speaks again before I can.

"Okay. Thank you, Mrs Joan," he says. "Must get on. I must."

And he is gone.

Gramma smiles into the space Tony just occupied. I am glad that I didn't manage to speak again. It is clear she is fond of him. And the last thing that a dying woman needs is to witness an argument over a few hundred pounds. I decide I'll ask him later. She waits until the door closes, and then reaches furtively into her cardigan pocket. She takes out something wrapped in paper napkins and passes it to me.

"Lemon drizzle cake," she says. "I stole it."

I take it from her and pull gently at the napkins to ensure that they don't take the cake with them.

"So, your wife?" she says. "Where were we?"

I tell her the story, right from the start.

Sara and I met about ten years ago. It was an online meeting, which I understand is not particularly rare nowadays. She contacted me directly, having tracked me down through various forums for missing people. She was at university at the time, and I was...well, I was kind of between jobs. We 'chatted' electronically for at least three months before we decided it may be a good idea to meet. Sara was studying law and as part of her course she got involved with old unsolved cases and possible miscarriages of justice. That type of thing.

We met for coffee at a motorway service station halfway between where she lived and I lived. Of course, by that time I had done my homework and through various social media platforms I now had at least an idea of how she looked (she later told me that she had done the same). I can't say that it was love at first sight because it didn't feel that way. In fact, I'm not fully sold on the idea of its existence. She looked different in person than online. She was pretty average in most ways: average height, average weight, average looks, average clothes, average, average, average.

But as we talked that afternoon, she became more and more attractive and less and less average. She spoke with true passion. Passion for life, passion for helping people, passion for making a difference. I was captivated. Even the way her mouth formed certain words thrilled me. She had a beautiful smile: perfect teeth and two large dimples in her cheeks which seem to frame her

(smile)

like brackets.

To the right of her mouth, she had another tiny dimple which only appeared when she pronounced words with a long 'e' vowel sound. Words like *sleep* and *please* and *dream*. I began to ask her questions that forced her to answer with one of those words, just so I could see it momentarily appear.

We sat in that service station drinking endless rounds of flat whites until the darkness captured the sun.

I don't believe in love at first sight.

But I certainly left in love.

The following year, Sara finished her law degree and immediately moved in with me. It made sense; after all, I am much closer to the city, where she could find work.

At first things were great. (How many times has that line been used?) I suppose when two humans choose to move in together, they are on their best behaviour. They straighten their shoes in the hall, they hang up their coats, they prepare fresh meals for one another, they squeeze toothpaste onto both toothbrushes. And that's what we did.

Prior to moving in together, we were in a long-distance relationship and only saw one another once or twice a week. This makes the maintenance of the relationship so much easier, as you can commit all your goodness to the days you spend together. That still leaves five or six days to be the real you. The one who is argumentative, irritable, sad, exasperated with life. The one who eats junk food, leaves towels on the floor, doesn't make the bed in the morning. That type of thing. So, it is fairly easy to get all the bad parts out in your own time and then present all the good traits when together.

After a golden period of maybe six months, maybe a year, we fell into a routine. Sara worked long hours at a large law firm in the city. She left early. She returned late. I continued to live off my inherited wealth, spending my days pretending to investigate my mum's disappearance whilst actually consuming a lot of films and television shows. Most of my knowledge about the world around me came from Hollywood.

I got past the stage where I could openly tell Sara that I'd spent all afternoon watching films. She would sigh or tut. Her eyes told me she was growing weary of the way I spent my days. The rejection from such small symbolism was too much to bear. It was easier to lie about my daily activities, and when possible weave the things I'd seen on screen into my life as if they had happened to me. It just made life easier. I'd dress about fifteen minutes before she returned.

The white lies enabled six years to pass fairly quickly. We were happy, I think, for the most part.

But I could tell that Sara's long working days clashed with my empty days of nothingness. It irritated her. And that irritated me. And so, when our relationship was stretched like pulled dough, we got married.

This worked for a while. A welcome distraction for us both. For another year, as a married couple, we returned to being on our best behaviour. I even got a job – and was introduced to MySnug – to appease her.

But if you keep stretching dough, it does eventually break.

I don't remember exactly when she told me she didn't love me anymore. It wasn't long ago. Perhaps a year or so.

At least she told me face to face that she was going, unlike my mother.

Gramma sighs.

I can't tell whether it's because of my story or the mention of my mother. I'm never going to find out unless I ask. Time is short.

"Why did you sigh?"

Her forehead somehow makes room for another hundred lines.

"I'm just sad for you, Samuel."

"I'm sure there's more?"

"Well," she says, bending forward in her chair, her head and neck hunched. "Relationships nowadays, they just don't last. And from what you say, dear, you seemed to have everything. But" – she raises her crooked finger – "you young people look for a life of constant pleasure and try to avoid pain. You get trapped in a hopeless cycle that goes round and round, on and on endlessly. And this causes you to suffer greatly. You need to understand that pain is a part of life."

I'm interested. I take a bite of lemon cake. Whilst I chew, she sees an opportunity to continue.

"You young people, you're always wandering. Searching. Looking for more. You're never in the moment; instead you're looking at what happens after the moment. It's a cycle, Samuel."

I nod. I have to admit that it seems to make sense.

"And you described Sara and her moods, her ways, her ability to change and how you thought she'd be a different person."

"Yes."

"No matter how many times you polish an apple, it will always be an apple underneath."

I can't tell whom this comment is directed at. It could be me. It could be Sara. It could be my mum.

My guess is Sara, but it leaves me very uneasy about what Gramma is trying to say.

She dabs at the corners of her eyes, which have begun weeping. I notice a slight flickering in the thin skin of her eyelids, and she suddenly sinks back into her chair.

"I'm tired," she says.

They are not the words that I want to hear. I suddenly have a thousand questions that I want to ask her.

I watch as her eyes flicker, then gently close.

I wait until her breathing becomes deeper and I am as sure as I can be that she is asleep.

Her eyes continue to flicker, as if watching my every move from beneath her eyelids.

When I leave, I am still not sure whether she was watching or not.

Chapter 20

18.12
-16.48

Chapter 21

I log out of MySnug and check the time. It's just after midnight. I stretch and slide my chair backwards. I leave it spinning and it is still moving as I reach the door. Then, as I enter the hall, I stop in my tracks. I can hear her clearly from here. Her voice sounds crisp and bright, as it always did. She sounds hopelessly happy, like a Disney character or children's television presenter.

Her voice tells me that she is 'Walking on Sunshine', and although I hate the sickliness of the song, I take a seat on the floor, my back pushed against the high skirting board.

Her voice is clear and chimes like Christmas bells. It is so close, she could be right next door, in the kitchen. But I know she isn't. I have been tricked too many times by her call. I've raced from room to room, following the voice, convinced I'll see her. Even years after her disappearance, I've somehow persuaded myself that she has returned and picked up where she left off (even though it is entirely illogical that anyone missing for a period of years would return singing the same song and resume cleaning duties instantly).

I tap my feet to her rhythm, and smile when she fills in the verse with mumbled gibberish or na-na-nas. And then, after one final rousing chorus where she tells me that 'it feels good' at least thirty times, the song draws to a close, and as it does she becomes more distant until, just like a bubble, the fantasy pops and her voice is gone.

I get to my feet and switch off the floor lamp in the hall. All is dark, aside from the shallow moonlight that pours like oil through the window on the stairs.

I brush my teeth and climb into bed. My body feels worn and tired, but my mind doesn't. It is just getting started. I know this feeling too well. My mind inserts itself into my reality just at the wrong time. It waits until everything else has been concluded for the day.

When all my daily tasks have been completed.

When I no longer need to move.

When I am lying down and comfortable.

When it is quiet.

And then, like the annoying guests at a surprise party, it reveals itself. *I'm here,* it cries. *You know me, your mind.* And its narrative unravels at the speed of a fighter jet. *I thought now everything was quiet, I might come out and well, have a catch-up with you. Y'know, run through the day, process the events that have happened, that type of thing. As you already know (because after all these are your thoughts, not mine), I always think it's better that we try to take a lesson from the day's experiences at the exact moment you're most tired. I see it as a learning curve. I can store some of the things we've experienced together just in case they come in handy in the future. Other things...well, they'll need much more analysis for us to come to any kind of conclusion. That's if we ever do. We've been together long enough to know we don't always come to a conclusion. In fact, it's rare. But I still believe there's value in trying to process things. Don't you?*

I roll over in bed, hoping the change of position might help me to sleep.

Don't you, Sam? Don't you think it's better to think these things through? Y'know, be more prepared?

My body feels physically exhausted. Like it needs to stop. Right now.

Sam, I was just saying, don't you think it's better to process these thoughts? Y'know, so we can both sleep more soundly?

I turn onto my stomach and kick one leg out from under the duvet. It instantly feels cold, so I pull it back under.

Sam?

Sam? Come on, don't be rude. We've got things to discuss. Things to (if you'll pardon the pun) put to bed. Come on...

I pull one pillow over my head, as if covering my ears could ever have an effect on a voice that

I hear from inside my head rather than outside. I just want to sleep now.

Sam, come on now. (My mind suddenly sounds more assertive, less playful.) *You know you'll relent eventually. I mean, it's not as if I'm going anywhere, is it?*

I snigger out loud, seconds after I hear my mind laugh.

Chance would be a fine thing, it says.

This continues until through my window I see the blue hour begin. This was always my dad's favourite part of the day, that time of twilight between the close of night and the opening of morning. In fact, he liked it so much that he would wake us on our weekend camping trips simply to see it. Whilst Tom and I would have preferred to be wrapped up warm in our sleeping bags rather than staring directly into the cobalt, it was easier to play along. We spent our childhoods carefully walking along the cliff edge where putting a foot wrong would take us directly over the sheer drop to our dad's temper. I became an expert in faking enthusiasm. I have to say it's served me well since.

That's all very nice. But that's a memory. How do we deal with today?

Sam?

Sam?

Gramma.

That's better. That's more like it. Now what about her? What's the issue?

I haven't always had it in for Gramma. In fact, when we were younger she was the saviour of our 'family' days. Each and every Sunday we would go over to Gramma and Gramps' bungalow for Sunday lunch.

Mum, Dad, me and Tom.

Gramma and Gramps.

We'd spend the afternoon there. Come home early evening. On the face of it, this seems like a fairly regular routine for most families. Roast beef. Washing up. Tea. Biscuits. Open fire plus the heating on (set by someone to cremation levels). The kind of heat that makes the elderly somnolent and the young drip with sweat – and in the case of my parents, a good way to sleep off the excesses of the night before. Tom and I would be left playing silently with plastic cowboys or drawing and colouring, always vigilant that the scratching of the felt-tips wasn't enough to wake Gramps. Or my father for that matter.

From memory, Mum would be the first to fall asleep. I can only assume in hindsight that it was a far better option than being awake in the same room as my dad and my gramps. Obviously, the weight of her decision to marry into this family wore her down. Tom and I didn't begrudge her sleeping away Sunday afternoons; after all, she cared for us pretty much exclusively during the week.

Again with the benefit of twenty years of self-analysis, it is clear that nothing would ever have made Gramps happy. Of course, we would do our best to make him proud. At least then genetically he had contributed to something positive.

I have made excuses for too many years now that the war affected him in ways that we cannot understand. He met my gramma six months before the war began. As he left for overseas, he promised her that he would marry her on his return. This statement could sound beautifully romantic.

Or,

an alternative view (one that, knowing Gramps, I feel far more comfortable with), is that he simply wanted to trap her. To have someone waiting for him; someone whom he knew, given her Methodist background, would be faithful until his return.

And he did return.

Seven years later, he walked back into the remnants of the bombed city that Gramma had watched collapse around her as she waited patiently for him. It's impossible to say that the man who returned was not the man who left, because Gramma had only had maybe a dozen dates with him before war came calling. She didn't really know the stranger who left or the stranger who returned.

They married after a month, and my father arrived ten months later.

The Gramps who returned was damaged in ways that most soldiers are after witnessing horrific scenes of human degradation and destruction. His mood was the driving force for everything in our family. On the good days (which were rare) he might share a story or a dark joke. He might even pull out a bag of boiled sweets and offer us one. He would tell us of other men in his regiment and what happened to them. He might tell us about stealing turnips from German farms or conquests (of the non-war type) in the small villages dotted around the countryside where they were stationed. The villages where the young local widows were too scared for themselves and their children to do anything but go along with the requests of Gramps and his battle-weary troops.

But for the most part, it was difficult to feel anything but contempt for Gramps. Nothing that Gramma did was ever good enough. At Sunday lunch, he would sit back in his chair (the only dining chair with arms) and allow Gramma to serve him. We would all watch silently as he grunted instructions to her.

More roast potatoes.

Too many carrots.

For God's sake, don't let the peas touch the mashed potato.

Pour the gravy on the meat first. How many times do I have to tell you?

Once his plate was full, he would close his eyes and we would all follow suit. Then he'd say grace, offering empty thanks for the food in front of him. The moment the word 'Amen' left his mouth, his eyes would flick open and, like a hungry jackal, he would slowly eye each face around the table. Almost licking his lips in anticipation of devouring each of us. Nobody around that table ever made eye contact with him. Instead, Tom and I would pretend to adjust the napkins on our knees, waiting for his stare to pass. His face – bitter as a winter lemon – told the same story to each of us. The story of a man disappointed with the people who surrounded him each week. A man who would rather be anywhere but here.

And then he would begin to eat, while my mum helped Gramma to serve everyone else. He would bark out complaints (and exclusively complaints) whilst the rest of us waited hungrily for our food.

The meat was too chewy. *You've left it in too long again, haven't you?*

The sprouts were overcooked. *Why does this happen every week? Can't you get anything right?*

The sweetcorn was cold.

The Yorkshire puddings were burnt / too crunchy / too soft / the wrong shape / the wrong size.

It was an exercise in stripping down every ounce of dignity left in my gramma. And she would apologise for each and every complaint he made, reassuring him that it wouldn't happen again. That she would try harder. Her face remained staunch, but it was impossible to think that there were not tears welling just behind her eyes. On many occasions, I saw her being comforted by my mother whilst they washed the dishes after dinner.

It was all Gramma could do. Any argument from her, or even a flash of emotion, would cause Gramps to bang his fist on the table – the volume of his voice would make Tom and I jump even though we knew it was coming. On rare occasions, Gramma would have to clean his dinner from the wall and carpet, on her hands and knees collecting gravy-soaked shards of porcelain and part-chewed carrots while he slept next door.

When he had finished his meal, he would slide his chair back, leave the table and walk into the lounge to recline his chair. No words were spoken. There would be a brief collective moment where all of our breathing returned to normal. Then Gramma would begin asking questions about work, school, my dad's car – anything to try to make Gramps' performance less relevant. Now and again, she would make some witty comment and we'd all use our hands to cover our mouths and hold in our laughs until we were sure they wouldn't come out too noisily for Gramps, who lay horizontal only a matter of feet away.

After dinner, and clearing up, Gramma would lay a tray with tea and a large plate of homemade biscuits on the strange eight-legged hexagonal coffee table in the centre of the lounge.

If Gramps was to be believed, the tea was always weak, the biscuits like granite.

Following afternoon tea and whilst three-quarters of the adults slept, Gramma would get down on the rug with Tom and me, and we would play silent word games and colour in pictures of astronauts and Robin Hood and dragons. Although the room was silent, Gramma was still able to make us smile, her raised eyebrows, cheeky winks or whispered jokes quickly turning into a frown if she feared we may make a little too much noise.

All of this changed, though, I suppose, when everything changed.

You see, I haven't always had a vendetta against Gramma. Not at all. As I said, she was the only shining light on those grey Sundays.

It was what she did after Mum disappeared that caused everything to change again. Something unforgivable.

I turn off my lamp and turn on the main light using the switch by my bed. All hope of sleep is now lost. I take a pen and paper from the drawer and decide to make a list of things I want to ask Gramma.

Before it really is too late.

Chapter 22

I am up and showered just in time to attend a mandatory two-hour meeting regarding our current projects. The virtual room is full, with thirty-seven attendees. I'm mildly cheered by the fact that I'm not making virtual coffees for them all. I am also pleased with the number of attendees as this means that the likelihood of me having to speak is very low.

20.36
-14.24

The meeting ends, and I count myself fortunate that the virtual room was filled with half a dozen individuals whose only strategy is to progress further up the corporate ladder. That meant that their voices echoed through the speakers constantly and thus when the meeting timed out I had managed not to speak. Not one sound. It was Sunday afternoons all over again.

I am glad I have got a head start on the week and have worked more hours than I am scheduled for. This frees up a little time to add to the list of questions that I started earlier this morning.

I sit on the floor and begin to leaf through the unsorted papers, placing them in the correct order as I go. The light from the sun forces itself through the branches of the trees outside, creating a fire-like dance on the office wall. I am captivated by the reflective shapes that grow and shrink, twist and turn. Then I return to my work. Eventually, my neck begins to ache, and I am drawn to the handwritten pages prepared and annotated by Gramma for no other reason than the beauty of them.

There are more than twenty pages, each one written in clear blue ink. My Gramma's script-style writing is neat and compact, the words perfectly straight across the page. I begin on page one, which seems like a sensible place to start, and read through each carefully. Gramma notes things my father said to her, things the police said to her, and her own thoughts and observations. In some ways the pages form more of a diary than anything else, but I am hopeful that this time around I may just find something that helps.

By the time I reach page eight, I have written down seven further questions to ask Gramma. The most interesting note covers a conversation with an investigating officer who tells Gramma that my mum was seen alive and well two days after she went missing about forty miles north of here. Not only was she spotted at a motorway service station, but the witness actually spoke to her. It appears, if the papers are to be believed, that the witness knew my mother from many years ago and it was a surprise for them both to reconnect. Gramma notes that: 'Sandra's demeanour was described as evasive, almost aloof. This came as a shock to [the witness] as Sandra had always been smiling, bubbly and happy to chat.' It appears that the conversation was brief, with my mum getting into a silver car moments after she met [the witness] with a man she seemed to know.

I continue to read through the papers, attaching Post-it notes where necessary and furiously scribbling down more questions on my list.

Somehow the dancing shapes bring me hope.

Like they are a sign of something good.

Chapter 23

It is mid-afternoon by the time I reach St Dymphna's. The sun has been substituted with drizzly rain. I am glad to reach the door. I push the bell and wait.

Nothing.

I am about to push the button again when I feel a hand on my shoulder. A heavily inflected voice states: "Mr Samuel."

I recognise the voice and turn quickly, my heart pumping double-time. It's Tony. He obviously recognises something in my face, as he says, "Sorry. Sorry. I didn't mean to make you, er, have fear."

My heart slows.

"It's okay," I say, "not a problem."

"I didn't mean for you to jump."

He shuffles past me and swipes a plastic pass, which allows him to enter the building. He holds the door open for me to walk through and that's when I notice his coat. It's a black puffer jacket which shines with the gloss of a bin bag. I recognise the brand stitched into his shoulder and chest and I know it's not cheap. The door clicks shut behind him.

"It's okay," I assure him. Then, as he passes me again, I add, "Nice coat? Is it new?"

He looks down at himself as if to check that he is indeed wearing a coat. He looks back up. "Yes, er, new. eBay," he says.

"Very nice," I say, nodding, "very nice."

I push open the door to my gramma's bedroom and as usual she is in her chair, seemingly staring at the wall. She doesn't turn when I enter.

"Hi, Gramma," I say.

"Not you again," she says sharply, then she smiles. "Come here, Samuel."

I walk over to her chair and lean down to give her a hug. She is too old and probably too tired to return the hug. She lifts her head and turns her cheek toward me to kiss. I do what she expects, and smell irises as I move away. Then I sit on the bed and take my list out of my pocket.

She eyes me warily as I unfold it.

"Is it a quiz?" she says. She winks and a tear runs down her cheek instantly. She dabs it with her tissue. She is about to speak again but thinks better of it.

"Kind of," I reply.

I straighten the creases across my knee and hold up the pages so she can see.

"Are they questions for me?" she says. "Because –"

"It's okay, I'm going to read them to you."

"That should be fine, dear."

"Good, okay, no time like the present. So, right, the first question. Did Mum ever talk about leaving Dad?"

She closes her eyes slowly and holds them that way for a few seconds before opening them again. Her eyes are running again.

"Samuel," she says quietly, "I'm old. My memory isn't good. I'd prefer not to spend my final days talking about this subject. It'll only end in heartbreak."

"But I need to know, and frankly, you're the only real hope I have –"

"We don't want to rake that up again, Samuel."

This is a statement.

I repeat my previous sentence, abridged: "Gramma, I need to know."

"Do you remember what happened last time we talked about this?"

I do.

It involved raised voices. Shouting. Swearing. An incident. A fall. Words that sliced through me like a scimitar. Uncensored words which to this day have left invisible scars all over my skin. Over my being. I felt like I was being massacred that day. 'Home truths' is what I remember Gramma calling them. Whatever words were spoken that day, they were the last we were to exchange for nearly twenty years. Up until, well, a day or two ago.

"I know we disagree, I know that, Gramma. But that's not what I want from you. We won't agree, but I just need to feel I've done everything. Y'know, for Mum."

She stares at me.

"I hear her singing. I feel her around me. I feel that the whole story hasn't been told. There's something. Please. I just want to hear your answers. I have to find the truth."

And that is effectively it. All I want is an end to this nightmare. I just want to be able to rest. I want Mum to be able to rest.

I feel my eyes begin to fill.

"Okay," she croaks, and I think I see her trying to force words around the lump in her throat. "But if we disagree, we move along. We don't argue. I can only tell you my view. It might not be right, but it is what I believe."

I wipe a tear from my cheek and take a deep breath. "Thank you," I say.

We talk for the next two hours, working our way methodically down my list of questions. Some are easily answered with caveated one-sentence answers. These answers are 'to the best of her knowledge'. Or 'if her memory serves her correctly'. Or 'it's a long time ago, Samuel'. Others she simply doesn't know. There is obvious confusion over dates and times and she has difficulty recalling the names and indeed faces of some of the police officers and detectives. I record everything on my phone. You never know.

I can tell that she is tiring. A slight tic has developed in the corner of her mouth – it seems to be a physical reaction to drawing memories from deep within her mind. Despite numerous sips of water from her tip-cup, I can tell from her voice that her throat is dry and she is having difficulty forming the words.

There is a light knock at the door and Tony enters without waiting for a response. He has removed his coat and I notice pale yellow marks down the front of his smock.

"Hi. You're still here," he states, sounding surprised.

"I am," I say, smiling.

He turns to Gramma. "Mrs Joan, will you be eating dinner?"

I check my watch and I am surprised that it is nearly six o'clock.

"Pardon, dear?" she says, looking confused.

Tony repeats his question.

"Just a little," she says.

"Okay, I'll come for you in, say, five minutes. I'll go and get the wheelchair."

He nods, and pulls the door closed behind him.

I take Gramma's hand in my own. It feels cold to touch. I am struck by just how slight, how thin, it feels. It is nothing more than a collection of the most fragile, tiny bones held together simply by the skin wrapped around them. I feel nothing in the way of fat or muscle. She looks down at her hand and then up at me. I smile.

"Thank you for today," I say. "It can't have been easy."

She smiles as she dabs her eye.

"I really appreciate it."

I stroke her hand and feel the loose skin gather at her knuckles.

"There's more, isn't there?" she asks.

"More?"

"More questions," she says.

"Yes."

"Then come tomorrow," she says.

"Are you sure?"

"Yes. We don't have long, do we?"

Again, I find myself pushing back the small lump that has developed in my throat. "No," I reply honestly.

"Okay. It's a date."

I gently place her hand back on her lap and open the wardrobe. "Which one today?" I say, holding up three different cardigans on hangers.

She decides on a mauve one, which instantly strikes me as a bad idea just before dinner.

I wait until Tony reappears and help him to move Gramma into the chair. We swap her cardigan at the same time, and I make a point of checking the pockets before I neatly fold the dirty one and place it on the bed. I make sure that Tony notices me doing so, and make sure he sees me putting the screwed-up tissue and bits of fluff in the bin. I kiss Gramma lightly on the side of her head and promise that I will arrive after breakfast the next morning.

I reach the door first, and as I pull the handle my gramma says quietly, "Oh, Samuel, I almost forgot. Will Thomas come to see me?"

"I don't know," I say.

It's as honest as I can be.

Chapter 24

It is after one in the morning when I finally finish work for the day.

After arriving home, I had decided to simply plough through the avalanche of emails waiting for me. I figure that if I get enough hours on the clock, then I can free up more time to spend with Gramma. Time becomes increasingly important when your main concern has a very real and very finite end-date.

I realise that Gramma has seemed to improve over the last few days and wonder if my presence has given her a new reason to stay alive. A new reason to be. I also wonder whether Tom's presence would have a similar effect and perhaps keep her going that little bit longer.

I check my diary for the rest of the week and discover that I have no further mandatory meetings. To an extent, my time is my own. I log off my machine, pleased that I am closing in on my regulation hours so early in the week.

26.00
-9.00

I pick up my phone for what seems like the hundredth time this evening. Whilst I've been working, it has exercised by vibrating its way around my desk for most of the evening. Each time I've tapped the screen, it's been the same number. Each time I've chosen not to take the call, pushing the button on the side to silence him.

I delete the thirteen missed calls, but I am surprised to see that he has left me one voicemail. He never does this. He says that it's a waste of his credit. That he doesn't get charged if he can cut off the call just as it connects. I switch the phone to speaker and press play.

There is a slight crackle and the sound of metal hitting a solid surface, maybe the floor, and then his voice. He spits the words like poisonous bullets, each one packed with venom.

"Sam. Where the fuck are you? I've rung fuck knows how many times. I want to know how your gramma is. Have you even seen her today? Have you visited? You do know she's dying, don't you? And you can't even give up the time to see her. You can't even give up the fucking time to answer my call. It's just fucking selfish. But that's how it's always been, isn't it? Think about yourself, Sam. Fuck everyone else."

I listen to the message again, pleased to be armoured from his words by proximity. I would like to be able to react to his message and tell him where to go, but I already know that I am not able. I never have been.

Whilst Mum was still here, my role was to protect her from my father's angry outbursts, which would reduce us all to tears, sometimes before he had even opened his mouth. Initially, I would try to get in the way of their disputes, to be the barrier that she so clearly needed. After a while I realised this was pointless. The arguments may cool at that moment, but later, when Tom and I were in bed, they would flare up five times hotter than before. We would hear my father's voice, punctuated by the sound of things being broken, through the floor beneath us.

And so I no longer got involved. Instead, I hid as close by as possible and listened. I listened to the words he used. I listened to the things that upset him, and I did everything I could to stop those things happening.

If our toys were out around the house, I'd tidy them.

If our shoes weren't straight in the hall, I'd neaten them.

If the pots in the sink lingered for more than half an hour, I'd wash them.

If.

If.

If.

I'd do everything that needed to be done to stop my mother being bullied and shouted at and mistreated. I spent my life in reconnaissance, watchful of my father, the enemy. Always alert, always surreptitiously waiting and ready for instant action where necessary.

It rarely worked, of course. It didn't matter how many things I did to appease him, there would always be something else – the next thing – that irritated him enough to unleash himself on Mum.

As the eldest, it was me whom Mum turned to. I was just old enough to be her confidant. The person she could offload to. It was clear from what she told me that she had nowhere else to turn. Dad had long ago cut off her friends. Of course, she always waited to speak to me when Dad wasn't around. For him to see her cry or even be upset around me or Tom was enough to make it all start again.

But when we were alone, she would stroke my hair and tell me that one day it would all be better. That one day it would be just the three of us and we wouldn't have to put up with it anymore. That we would run somewhere far away and live our lives without him.

And it was that promise that I clung to each and every time the house exploded spectacularly with his sickening words that burned through each of us like molten lava.

Chapter 25

I am up early and arrive at the nursing home just after nine thirty. Susan lets me in without speaking and then scurries off – in one door and out of another – like a rat in a maze.

The third door on the corridor is open, and as I pass I hear a groan, which causes me to stop. I take a breath and then a step backwards. The bed is occupied again. A man lies facing the door, his features partially hidden by the pillow. I can see that his eyes are closed. His skin is dark and creased and his complexion is like a walnut. The artificial light forms an ominous white square that reflects on the top of his head. I wait for a moment to be sure that the moan came from him. I can hear furniture being moved on the floor above.

The man opens his eyes and I watch as his pupils focus. He then lifts his head slightly and pulls a painful-looking smile. I smile back, unsure whether he can actually see me.

Then he lifts his arm a few inches above the blanket and outstretches his fingers. He motions toward me and I get the feeling he is trying to wave.

A moment later, his eyes close again and his arm drops silently back down.

I stand and watch him for another few minutes. I want to make sure that he is okay. He doesn't moan again.

"Samuel!" Gramma says. "Well, what a lovely surprise."

I can't tell if she is joking with me or she had actually forgotten I was coming to see her. I flash a brief smile so she knows her joke isn't lost on me. I suppose that the last thing you want is to lose your audience when delivering what could be one of your last jokes on this earth.

Today, she looks the brightest I've seen her, a slight, almost mischievous glint in her otherwise matt eyes.

"In the top drawer," she says, pointing. "I have something for you."

I open the drawer to tights and bone-white underwear.

"At the bottom," she says, "beneath the drawer liner."

I delve beneath her underwear and locate the drawer liner, which is patterned with flowering lavender.

"Do you have it?"

I pull the brown envelope from the bottom of the drawer and hold it up.

"This?" I say.

"That's it." She smiles and asks me to pass her the envelope.

I watch as her bony fingers struggle to pull the inserted flap from within the envelope. Every movement is laboriously slow. I want to take it from her and help, but it seems more courteous to let her go on struggling. I am worried that taking such tasks from her will only serve to highlight the pointlessness of her existence and accelerate her demise. The envelope is finally open and I watch her hand slip weakly inside. She pulls out a small number of square Polaroid photographs and passes them to me.

I thank her and take a moment to look at the pictures. The first picture shows me, my mum and my brother. We are at a picnic and I instantly recognise which one. Tom lies across the picnic blanket, his feet chopped off on the far right of the picture, his head on my mother's outstretched thigh. My mother's bare feet point to the photographer. Her eyes look deserted, as if she is looking into a camera behind the one taking the picture. Her stare reminds me of battle-weary soldiers. Her mouth says nothing of how she feels. I am off to the left, a good foot separating me and my mother. I am smiling and my head is resting lazily to the left as if someone has told me to move in closer. I don't know why, but seeing the pineapple-coloured fields and blue sky in the space between us resonates. I have to take a breath.

The next picture shows Tom and me standing at the top of the garden. We are near a huge pile of soil, and from the colour of our clothes and faces, it looks like we have already summited it. We look similar in age to the picnic picture. Maybe a little older.

The last two pictures show my father with me and Tom. The first of the two is faded and old and the real colours have fled, replaced by gold where yellow once was, maroon for red, blue for green. I look about seven, which means Tom is two, maybe three. At the front of the frame, I kneel on one knee, proudly displaying a football that I grip with both hands. In the background, my father, with long sideburns and longer hair, rests on his muscular arms, his legs outstretched across the long blue grass. He is looking away from the camera. Tom sits on his knee, facing the camera. His mouth is wide, tears and snot have collected around his cheeks and upper lip, and his cheeks are a deep maroon colour.

The final photograph is much more recent. Well, relatively. Again, it shows me, my dad and Tom. This time we are much older. I'd guess I am sixteen – my Teenage Mutant Ninja Turtles t-shirt time-stamps me. Tom is around eleven. My dad stands in the middle, and I am struck by his resemblance to the Gramma who sits in front of me now. His face is thin and drawn. His dark hair hangs limply across his forehead, the pink of his scalp now evident. His eyes are almost black, both in his pupils and the two large circles around them. His expression can be summarised in one word: defeat.

He seems to be using what little strength he has left to grip Tom and me around the upper arm, pulling us in toward him. Our spare arms hang obsolete by our sides. None of us are smiling.

I look up at Gramma and try a smile. I get the feeling that she has been watching me study the photographs.

"So?" she croaks.

I'm not sure what she wants me to say. I pass the photographs back to her, but she refuses and instead passes the empty envelope to me. "They're for you," she says, "to keep."

I thank her and put the photographs away. I don't know how I feel at this moment. I feel sad and happy and choked up and angry. I am fortunate she breaks the silence.

"Is it time for the interrogation to start again?" She winks.

I smile. "I'll make tea first," I say.

Chapter 26

Gramma sips her tea and rests the saucer on her lap.

We have been speaking about the past, the times before I was born and after. We have covered her childhood and teenage years. I've scribbled down rough notes to accompany our conversation and ticked off questions that she has answered. Although the body that carries her has all but withered away, her mind remains alert. Conscious. Aware.

We talk about her marriage and the birth of my father. She tells me for the first time that my father had a sister, who was 'born dead', as Gramma pointedly puts it. As I write the two words down alongside one another, I am shaken by how they look on the paper.

We talk about Gramps. About his war heroics and the various medals and awards he received for his bravery, his gallantry and his leadership of men. She tells me of people whom he risked his own life to save. She tells me of shells exploding and bursting his eardrum, bullets that lodged in straw bales inches before they would have lodged in Gramps. I have to say I am impressed by the stories, and they highlight to me that if I were ever in that position, I would undoubtedly be a coward. I let her tell his stories because I can see it brings her joy. She yawns and removes the tissue from her sleeve. As she wipes her eyes, I see my opportunity.

"Do you think that's why he was, er…" I pause, careful to choose my words. "…like he was?"

"Pardon?" she says.

I can't read her tone, and I immediately curse my attempt at sensitivity, which came across as stilted and vague. I take a short breath and try again.

"Do you think his wartime experiences made him the way he was?"

"Of course, dear," she says, the corners of her mouth upturned. "I'm sure war and seeing what he saw would change any of us."

My heart is beating more quickly. I am sure I can feel it moving toward my throat. I try again.

"I suppose what I'm trying to say is…well, Gramps, he wasn't…he wasn't exactly known for his kindness. I always felt –"

"He was very kind. And generous. He would help anybody at the church."

I decide to continue. "I always felt that he didn't like any of us. Me or Tom or Mum, or even Dad. I always felt we weren't good enough. Like we were a hindrance to him. An annoyance. A disappointment."

She blinks quickly and looks at a space above me.

"It was like everyone, including you, was scared of him."

"Those were different times..." she says. Her voice sounds a little stronger. A little more assertive. Whilst I consider whether to draw attention to her glaring display of stating the bloody obvious, she continues.

"Life was different then. We didn't have what you young people have now. Our hopes and ambitions were so much more grounded. Things were different, Samuel. It didn't really matter what I expected from life, but rather what life expected of me."

I nod.

"Like so many others, your gramps brought home memories that he couldn't rid himself of. Death and blood flooded into his everyday life. And he couldn't control that. Each day was like waiting for a pan to boil over."

"But is that any reason to be so mean to everyone? Including you."

She shakes her head and tells me that she doesn't know the answer to that. She tells me that she never thought of him as mean. That she felt he was protecting her and the family; that after the horrors he had seen, he couldn't cope with any more loss. Pushing us all to one side was not meanness but rather self-protection. Self-insulation against the cold hand of death. She always felt loved by him, even if he couldn't express it to her.

I don't know what to make of this. It still seems far simpler to me to smile at people rather than criticise them. I decide to park the conversation. There are more things I want to ask, but they'll have to wait. And I must be careful to broach these whilst Gramma is still happy to (and more importantly, able to) talk.

"You want to ask about your mother," she says.

She's right.

I nod.

"Well, ask," she says. "Time has moved on since, well, since our altercation. I'm too old and too tired to argue."

She coughs and I can hear the sputum partially separate from the inside of her throat. I imagine it hanging like a pendulum. She holds the tissue to her mouth and tries to cough it free.

"Please do ask me," she says, again unsuccessfully trying to clear her throat. I can hear the spit pendulum vibrating lightly with each breath.

"Okay." I glance at my list. "You and Mum seemed to get along?"

"Yes, of course. Sandra was beautiful, inside and out. I told your dad she was out of his league. A lovely person." There is a rasp in her voice, like a small insect is trying to break free from each word.

"So you weren't pretending for Dad's sake?"

She frowns. "No, of course not. I loved," she corrects herself, "*love* her very much to this day."

"Where did she go?" I ask.

She coughs again, and I pull a fresh tissue from the box on the small table and pass it to her. For a moment she is unsure what to do with the old, crumpled ball of tissue. I take it from her hand and try to ignore how damp and sticky it is as I drop it into the bin.

"I don't know, Samuel. Really I don't."

"But you'd guess…"

She turns her head to the window, as if looking out into the world will somehow help her to focus on my mum's exact location. There is a long, long silence.

(Like this)

Then she turns back to me and speaks, her words carefully considered.

"I am sorry to say this, but I think she left you. Just like the note said. She left you and Tom because she couldn't cope."

"With us?"

"With your father. With the amount of wine they were both drinking. With life."

"Would she have left us?"

"If she thought it was in your best interests –"

"To leave us with Dad?!"

"I think she knew that I'd be there for you. He was driving her into the ground. He controlled her. Criticised everything she did. I think she left to save herself."

"What about me and Tom?"

"I don't know," she rasps. "Is it selfish to save yourself?"

I don't know the answer to this either. My mind begins to race. I feel fear burn the back of my throat.

"Why are you so sure that she just upped and left?"

"She was seen by at least three people in the week after she left. Three people who knew her. They can't all be mistaken."

"Three?" It's been a while since I read the information contained in the box, but I don't remember three. Two maybe, but three?

"Yes. It's all written down, dear. And she had reason..."

My mind accelerates again. Three witnesses?

She coughs loudly and I hear the spit snap. She swallows it.

"What reason?"

"Well, wouldn't you want to leave your father if you were married to him? I know I would."

I ignore the illegality of her statement (and the vivid picture my mind has just painted), instead choosing to understand the underlying meaning.

"So where did she go?"

"If I knew that, Samuel..."

"But how can you be so sure?"

"She left to start a new life. That's just my opinion. She left with the stranger at the services."

"The stranger?"

"Yes. The man she was seen with."

"So you don't think she's dead?"

"I don't know, now. Years have passed, so maybe. I just think at that time it's much, much more like Sandra to leave than anything else. She had more fire, more spark and fight in her. And she was bright, much brighter than Ray."

I suddenly feel strangely proud of my mother. She was bright and fought for what she believed in. I wonder whether this is where I get my ragged spirit from. But then, I am instantly angry. If Gramma is right, then my mum left us because she couldn't cope with the life she had chosen. Isn't that a coward's way out? Leaving her children behind is not showing fight. It's weak. Weak and hopeless. My mind is racing out of control like an empty car on a steep hill.

"Too bright to end up under a patio," Gramma says bluntly.

There is a knock at the door and Tony enters. He insists that Gramma goes for dinner, telling her that she needs it for her strength. He also tells her that he got into trouble for letting her skip lunch. Finally, she agrees, and Tony leaves for the wheelchair.

I am glad she's agreed. I'm tired. I've had enough for one day.

I just want to walk out into the crispness of the end-of winter evening and think about what she has told me. I also need to find out who the three people are. I kiss her on the cheek and thank her. She asks whether I'll be back in the morning and I tell her I will.

I pass Tony in the corridor outside my gramma's door. He raises his eyebrows to save himself the effort of saying hello again.

As I near the front door, I notice that the third door is still open. The bed is made and waiting.

And the man is gone.

Chapter 27

30.06
-4.54

It's well after nine by the time I have eaten and answered emails and opened and closed miscellaneous documents. My eyelids seem to be taking gravity a little too literally, my eyes are dry and my vision is obscured, like I am seeing the world through creased cling film. I consider everything that Gramma has told me, and although all I want is to sleep, I am acutely aware that time is against me.

I turn on the radio and get down on the floor. I am about to lift the lid from the box when my phone begins vibrating on the desk above me. I scramble across the floor and pull myself to desk height. I collect the phone, knowing already that it's my dad.

It's my dad.

I push the button and sink to the floor again, lying on my back. We go through the beeps and then I hear his voice. I listen for a moment and realise that he is speaking to someone else in the background. His voice is muffled, like he is covering the receiver, and I can't make out what he is saying. And then the sound becomes clearer, and his voice is directed at me.

"Sam," he booms. "Sam, you there?"

"Hi, Dad," I say quietly.

"Sam. That you? Sam?"

"Hi, Dad," I say a little more loudly.

"Where have you been?"

"When?"

"The last few days. I couldn't get hold of you. Where have you been? Have you been to see her? How is she?"

"I've been busy –"

He tries to cut me off, but I have the courage to speak over him.

"I've been busy. I've been to visit Gramma every day. Okay?"

"You have?"

"Yeah. Every day."

"Okay," he says, and for a moment, apart from the usual background noise, the line is silent. I think the revelation that I *have* seen Gramma so many times has cut him off at the legs and now he's not sure what to say. His prepared rant is now redundant.

"Okay," he repeats, "and how is she?"

"She's okay. Generally. She's awake. Sitting up. Talking."

"That's good," he says.

"She asked after Tom today…"

"Oh," he says.

"Just thought I'd better say. I'm gonna ask him to come up."

"Yeah, right," he says sarcastically. He could have added any number of criticisms and attacks on Tom's personality and lifestyle, but he doesn't. The silence is an empty basket full of our thoughts.

"Hmm," I say.

"Are you going to see her again?"

"Yep. Definitely. I'll go until, well, until…"

"Right. Good. Okay, I need to go."

"Okay. Bye."

I'm about to hang up, but I hear his voice increase in volume and then cut off. I pull the phone back to my ear.

"Sorry?"

He's gone.

I stare at the ceiling for a while, considering what Dad has just said to me. I know that he is right about Tom and it makes me wonder when exactly we lost him.

An obvious guess would be around the time that Mum disappeared. At that time, Tom was about seven. He was already a permanent attachment to my mother. You only need to look at the photos to confirm this. Wherever Mum is in a photograph, Tom is there. An arm wrapped around her thigh. A chubby hand in my mother's. His head on her lap. Always touching. That was Tom. He was conditioned that way. Mum probably felt she could protect him the most when she could physically feel him. It wasn't his fault.

As far as I can remember he had always been Mum's favourite. This is something that I accepted a long time ago. My therapist helped me through that particular conundrum. I don't think it was as simple as Mum liking Tom more than me. Not at all. It was far more subtle than that.

And anyway, doesn't the youngest always becomes the favourite, at least for a period of time? I had my time, before Tom (though it's hard not to be the favourite when there is only one to choose from). I understood that the youngest child requires far more time and effort from their parents, but in addition to this, I also knew that Tom needed something else.

Protection.

Around the clock protection.

And he needed it far more than I ever did, because of how destructive Mum and Dad's relationship had become by the time Tom was a toddler. I know this because I've unpicked it all. I've spoken about it endlessly in therapy. I think I got the impression from a fairly young age that Mum felt guilty about introducing Thomas Darte into a world of arguments, mental torture and absent love. I suppose she hoped that Tom's arrival may somehow reverse the downturn in her relationship with my dad. Instead of Mum and Dad being stranded out at sea and drifting further away, baby Tom arrived to miraculously reverse the tide and carry them back to the safety of the shore. Tom must have tuned into this early on, because he became one of those children who is always looking to the parent they trust the most.

And then, just at the time Tom was old enough to understand and adapt to the world he was born into, it was snatched away from him.

Forever.

Mum didn't just leave for a few weeks and then return.

Tom's world changed *forever*.

Can you imagine how that feels to someone who has spent their whole life making themselves feel safe by touching and being near the same person every single day? For that to be taken without any kind of explanation must have been catastrophic for him. And with no resolution, even to this day.

After Mum's disappearance, Tom was left with little chance. There was only Dad to turn to now.

Perhaps if my dad had stepped into Mum's shoes, Tom's life would have improved, but Dad had no time or, it seems, inclination to do that. Instead, Tom remained cast out to sea, bobbing on the surface of the water hundreds of miles from shore like a solitary plastic cup.

And so, as my eyes follow the coving around the ceiling for the tenth time, it is clear to me that we lost a large part of Tom when Mum vanished. The moment that Tom found the note and Mum's rings on the table, a piece of him broke off and drifted. Of course, this needn't have been permanent. There was still plenty of time for Tom to be fixed back together. But unfortunately, there was nobody there to do this.

Tom therefore became the Tom we have now. Mum would be heartbroken. And I know that Mum would never have left either of us in that position.

I begin sorting through the box of papers again. A few more hours and then I think I'll be ready at last to review them.

One.

By.

One.

By.

One.

By.

One.

Chapter 28

Blue light streams through the conservatory glass, waking me with its brightness. It takes me a moment to realise that I am outstretched on the office rug. My neck is sore, and I rub it as I pull myself into a sitting position. I check my phone. It's just before seven.

I don't know what time I fell asleep, but I do know from the neat piles in front of me that all the papers are now in some kind of chronological order. They remind me of an Olympic podium. The smallest pile, the bronze pile, covers the period from Mum becoming a missing person to the police becoming interested in my father. A period of about four weeks. The gold pile is at least five times higher than the bronze. This covers the time period from when the police targeted my father until his final arrest. The silver pile...well, that covers from the arrest until, I suppose, the present day.

I sigh. I know that the gold pile is the one that I need to spend the most time on. Although, from what Gramma told me, the pile covering just after Mum went missing is vital. Three people saw her days after it is alleged that she lost her life. Obviously, someone is mistaken.

I rub my neck and yawn.

I need to keep going. Against my better judgement, my hand lifts my phone and my thumb hits my favourites. And then the phone is ringing, and she is facing me, smiling. The photo on my screen is from a bar somewhere in Cyprus. A few years ago. A good holiday.

"Hi?" she says. In a word of just two letters, her tone ranges between confusion and that flustered, I'm-a-solicitor-and-I-am-far-too-important-and-busy-to-speak-to-you voice.

"Hi, it's me."

"I know," she says (add weary into the mix).

"Y'okay?"

"Yes. What's up, Sam?"

I tell her about my gramma. I tell her about the piles of papers in front of me. I tell her of the three witnesses. Only Sara knows this case as well as I do. Possibly, she knows it better. After all, it was what initially joined us. Ironically, it was probably what finally separated us.

She sighs.

"What's up?" I ask.

"It's seven in the morning, Sam. I'm getting ready for work."

I don't quite understand the relevance of this. A hanging silence fills the space between us like a hammock between trees.

"That means," she says, sounding more primary school teacher than solicitor, "that I don't have time for this right now."

"Okay," I say defensively.

"I'll call you later," she says.

"Tonight?" I ask.

"Later," she says.

"Okay."

"Oh, and Sam…"

"Yeah?"

"She definitely said three witnesses?"

"Yeah. Definitely."

"Okay."

Her photo disappears from the screen and I'm left wondering when I'll hear from her next. I check the clock and my thumb hovers over my contact list. I toy with the idea of ringing Tom to the extent that I push his number twice and then hang up before a connection is made. He is likely to be asleep and I don't really have any pressing reason to wake him right now. He'd probably tell me he'd passed out in Alice Cooper's flat or on a studio floor with Jon Bon Jovi. But we don't have much time.

I push the button and this time let it ring.

I listen to staccato silence as the phone tries to connect.

No answer.

I hang up and try again.

And again.

And again.

And again.

"What the fuck, Sam?"

"Tom, at last."

"I'm asleep, man."

"Yeah, I figured."

"What time is it?"

"Seven."

He sniffs. "What the fuck?"

"It's Gramma," I say. "She's asking for you."

"Okay," he says, as if he's processed the magnitude of my statement in less than a second.

"What does 'okay' mean?" I ask. "Like, 'okay, I'll come and see her' or 'okay, thanks for letting me know, but I'm not going to do anything about it'?"

"Huh?" he says. I know he uses this phrase to buy time. He wants me to repeat all of my last sentence, even though he heard it, so he has the chance to think of a response.

"You heard," I said.

"Sam, man. Sam, listen, how come you're suddenly bothered about Gramma? You fucking hate her, man."

It's my turn to need more time to respond.

"You gonna visit or not?"

"What?"

"You gonna visit Gramma?"

"Fuck. No. I don't know. I'll call you later."

And he's gone.

In the seconds it takes for me to ring him back he has switched off his phone.

I have no doubt that he won't call me later. That's just Tom's way. Escape. Escape. Escape.

Run into the sunset.

Don't turn around.

Keep running.

Chapter 29

I spend the next few hours reading through the bronze pile. It is in here, if anywhere, that I will find a reference to the information that Gramma divulged yesterday.

It doesn't take me long to find the full statement to the police from the person who saw Mum at a motorway services two days after she disappeared. The woman went to school with my mother. She knew her well, well enough to speak with her, and had seen her plenty of times over the years since they both left school, some thirty years earlier. The woman's statement has some additional details that don't feature in my gramma's beautifully scripted notes: that my mum was 'not her usual self' and seemed 'keen to leave', and that she left with a man the witness had never seen before in a 'silver sports car'.

I pull the statement from the files and put it to one side.

The very next page is another report from the same police officer, who notes that another witness was sure she saw 'Mrs Darte across the car park of the service station' on the same day. The woman knew my mother by sight as she had children attending the same school as Tom. Although she had never spoken to my mum, she recognised the back of her hair and coat from the view she had. She had mentioned to her husband that she had seen her when she got back in her car.

Again, I extract this page and begin to flick through the next ones.

Just then, my computer chimes, and MySnug tells me that I am due to attend an urgent two-hour meeting later that afternoon. It is mandatory. I check my watch. I have five hours until the meeting begins. I need to get moving.

30.54
-4.06

Chapter 30

Inside the care home, somebody pushes the buzzer and the magnetic lock on the door clicks open.

As I approach the first door on my left, Tony appears. His eyes are red.

"Hello, Mr Samuel," he says, pushing a smile through his frown.

"Are you okay?" I ask.

Tony immediately takes this as a prompt to push the balls of his palms into his eyes and rub them from side to side. "I'm sorry," he says.

"What for?"

He sniffs, pulls a handkerchief from his pocket and wipes carefully under each eye as if he is removing eyeliner.

"Tony," I say, trying to take authority over the conversation, "what's happened? Are you okay?"

"I'm fine. I'm good. It's okay. It's okay."

He sniffs again, and then pulls a beaming smile which couldn't look less happy. From behind him, Susan appears. I wasn't aware she was in the office. In fact, I wasn't aware there was room for them both in the tiny room.

"Morning," she smiles. There's a brief flash of her raised eyebrows aimed at Tony.

"You're okay, aren't you?" she asks him.

He nods.

"You can go home," she says. "It's okay."

He shakes his head.

"Well," she says, "if you're staying, get yourself cleaned up. It'll be lunch before we know it."

He nods and again tries unsuccessfully to smile before squeezing past her and disappearing back into the office.

She turns to me. "He gets very attached," she half-whispers. She must have noticed my slight frown as she continues, "Mr Sanderson. Top floor. He passed this morning. He and Tony were very close."

"Ah," I say, the confusion disappearing like a magician's assistant.

"Right, better get on," she says.

I decide that now is probably not the right time to enquire into the money that mysteriously left my wallet a few days before.

Gramma's chair is facing the window again, just as when we first met. It feels significant somehow.

I wish the back of the chair "Good morning" and remove my coat and lay it on the bed. A moment later it's clear why I got no response from the chair. It's empty. My eyes dart around the room, and then, just before I reach for the wardrobe handles, I stop myself – logic dominating – when I realise that a woman in her nineties is unlikely to be playing hide and seek.

I turn the chair so it faces the bed again and at that moment the door opens. Two staff members enter the room silently and ignore my "hi". They remove the cuddly toys from my gramma's pillow and sit them against the skirting board. Then they slide out the bed and begin pushing it through the open door. The door closes, then reopens instantly and another member of staff I've not seen before leads the way, though it looks strange as she is walking backwards. She holds the door open with her foot and guides a much taller bed into the room. Her colleague helps her to put it in position, where the previous one was, and then leaves.

"Er, what's happening?" I ask.

The woman finishes what she is doing and turns to face me. "Hi," she says. "I'm Jacqui. I'm St Dymphna's nurse."

I figure Jacqui is the same age as me. She has a warm face, a glow that has either come from overheating or strategic make-up. Her teeth are perfectly straight and perfectly white and remind me of two rows of Tic Tacs. She wears a small watch upside down on the opposite side to her name badge.

"Right," I say. My heart begins to beat a little faster.

"And you are?"

"Sorry, I'm Sam. Er, Gramma's... Joan's grandson. Joan is my gramma."

"Right, okay," she says. "Well, we've had your grandma under observation through the night. We were worried about her breathing. She was quite breathless early yesterday evening."

I nod, hoping it will elicit more information.

"We have an observation room where we can attach patients to the machines and monitor them a little better. As I say, we've watched her through the night."

"And how is she?" I ask.

Jacqui squeezes the muscles in her face, as if she has just eaten the tiny, bitter seed that is sometimes unexpectedly hidden in a mouthful of pilau rice. She then frowns.

"She's doing really well," she says, lowering her eyes and shaking her head. She turns to the bed. "Aren't you, Joan?"

There's no response.

It's only when Jacqui moves to the side that I realise that my gramma is in the bed. Before then, I simply figured that Jacqui was making the bed. I didn't realise that Gramma lay beneath the creased sheets. I am completely taken aback at the difference in her from the previous day. Jacqui turns back to me and performs an exaggerated jerk of the head in the general direction of the door.

I follow her lead, and a moment later we are in the corridor.

"Sorry," she says. "We're never quite sure how much they can hear."

"It's okay, I understand."

"So, I'm sure it's not a surprise to know that your grandma is very old and her body is beginning to slow down."

"Okay…"

"We've moved her onto the adjustable bed now to make her last few days more comfortable. We'll be in and out to change her and turn her regularly and, well, to administer her medication when she needs it."

"Okay," I say again, swallowing. *I'm sure Jacqui has seen plenty of people cry, but I'm not going to be one of them.*

"You said 'last few days'…" I'm about to ask a question but my voice trails off, because I know releasing more words will only release the lump in my throat. And then the tears.

Jacqui takes my lead. "Yes, I think we're in the last few days now. Perhaps three or four, but no more."

"Okay." I feed my lips between my teeth.

"I would just warn you," she says, "there's a high chance of aphasia now. She's tired. She's literally worn out."

It seems a strange phrase to use to refer to my gramma. Like comparing her to the cardigans that hang in her wardrobe.

"Aphasia?"

"It just means she may not be able to communicate now."

"Okay," I say.

"Listen, if you need anything, just say the word. Press the red buzzer on the bed. Nothing is too small. If you're worried, ring. We're here twenty-four hours a day."

I am not sure if she means to touch my hand as she passes me. I watch her walk down the corridor, considering whether I have anything else to ask her. She turns the corner and is gone.

I push the door open and re-enter Gramma's room.

Chapter 31

The bed is taller than I first thought.

I stand alongside it, my chest resting against the top bar of the metal frame which runs horizontally around all four sides. Staring at Gramma from above seems like an intrusion, like an emperor on high watching gladiators fight to the death from the best seats in the amphitheatre.

She is lying on an immaculate white sheet. Her top sheet is pulled down so it now only covers her feet. She looks lost inside the cage. She is lying on her side, and for the first time I see how she really looks beneath the cardigans and (in happier times) the cream blouses with faux-pearl buttons. Her white nightdress drowns her, like she has climbed inside the discarded remains of an obese ghost.

She is facing me, but her eyes are closed. I can see the track marks of the constant liquid from her eyes. Small pieces of what looks like salt or sand have gathered around the corners of her eyes. For a moment I am tempted to gently scratch them off, but I don't want to wake her. Her mouth is open, her breathing both low and slow. Her top lip vibrates with every push of air, the small black hairs bending and standing like trees in a hurricane. Each push of air is accompanied by a slight click which seems to come from her throat. As if someone is registering each breath with a push of their thumb, counting down until there are no more.

Her arms are long and thin and it is actually possible to see the shape of her bones beneath the spent skin that hangs limply over them. The skin is wrinkled and dotted, like a plucked bird. It spreads slightly on the sheet beneath and the contrast of white on white only gives the skin an emptier, more pallid look. She is so pale, so fragile, that I feel if I looked closely enough, I could see right through her skin. I am only just able to tell where her skin ends and the sheets begin.

Her nightdress is slightly lifted, just above her knees, which stick out from her thin legs like two bruised apples. I realise now just how little of her is left. The muscle and fat are all but gone. Her heart is now pumping and distributing oxygen to little more than a shell of a person.

I am also struck by how lost and small I feel in this environment. My only experience of this is watching actors in films sit alongside their loved ones as they lay in a coma or close to death in hospital. I try to pull into my mind the actions they took. Some held their loved one's hand. Some continued to talk, in the hope that their loved one could still hear them. Some were quiet and provided comfort through touch, stroking the back of the hand, stroking hair, that type of thing. Others sobbed silently, desperately trying to muster some final strength from their rapidly depleting stocks. I seem to remember a couple throwing themselves dramatically on the floor, but that doesn't fit for me. After all, it's not about me.

All I know is that I don't know what to do.

I suppose I should just do what comes naturally. The problem is that I don't know what is natural. And so instead I freeze, staring at Gramma until my eyes sting like hers do.

It is only when my neck begins to ache from straining to see her over the bars that I decide to move position. I collect the rabbit and two teddy bears from against the skirting board and place them on the end of the bed near her feet, so she can see them should she wake. I don't want her to feel alone. Then I pull her chair to the head of her bed and sit. From here I can just see her, though the vast majority of my view is taken by the edge of the thick mattress.

I am angry that I have been left with the responsibility of guiding Gramma through her final phases of life. This is not my choice. I now have to decide – on my own – how to make these last few moments as perfect as possible for her. I have no guidance, I have no frame of reference. I can't ask her how she wants me to be, because she is unable to answer.

I am left simply guessing.

Like so many things in my life.

It was soon after Gramps died that Gramma moved in with us. I don't remember much about Gramps passing away, because frankly, in hindsight, I didn't care. I didn't care that his death would upset my father; it felt at the time that anything and everything would upset my father, and therefore to me the death of his father was just another thing.

Yawn.

Mum had already been missing four years by this time, and therefore I wasn't worried that Dad may take Gramps' death out on me or Tom. We were already pretty much living that experience every day anyway.

I don't know whether we expected Gramps to die. I don't remember there being any conversations or discussions leading up to it – just Gramma sitting Tom and me down and telling us that she had sad news. There were no tears or outpourings of emotion. I clearly remember that evening I met with friends on Beggar's Path and drank cheap cider and smoked joints at the Lightning Tree until well into the night. I told them my gramps had died, and we gulped back mouthfuls and raised invisible glasses to the sky in his memory. That was about the extent of my grief. And then we spent the evening laughing.

It hadn't occurred to me that Gramma may move in with us at that time. But in hindsight, it was an obvious move. She was now alone, her lifetime companion taken from her. My father was also alone, and I think the hope was that Gramma's arrival would make a much-needed change in the family dynamic. Gramma would bring a feminine touch to the home. She could cook and clean for us, which would benefit her and keep her busy, rather than spending long evenings alone making dinner for one and dusting and re-dusting her furniture endlessly.

I think my father also hoped that Gramma's arrival would somehow help to calm Tom, who was rapidly descending into completely-out-of-control. By this time he was eleven maybe just turned twelve. It was clear within a couple of weeks of his starting high school that he was going to need some very strong persuasion that attending his classes was worthwhile. Within a few months, he chose instead to spend his days alone. After breakfast, he would wait until Dad left for work and then change back out of his uniform and spend all day strumming his guitar. On the rare days when Dad was at home, Tom would leave for school and spend the day in the local woods or wandering the fields.

I must admit I did little to help the situation. Nothing at that time made sense, and I had enough to deal with without trying to act like some sensible big brother. To be honest, I didn't care whether he went to school or not, as long as he was happy. Which, of course, he wasn't.

Most evenings descended into screaming arguments between Tom and Dad. Tom had maybe been found with weed in his room or been spotted drinking in the woods by some dog-walker who had contacted my father. Tom had attended school that day, but sworn at a teacher and flipped a desk, before being suspended from the school again. Tom had been stealing money from Dad again. That type of thing.

It wasn't as though I wasn't doing all the same things; I was just older and far wiser than Tom as far as getting caught was concerned. My actions were equally as nihilistic, just a little more subtle; nihilism with the volume turned down. I suppose I considered trying to help Tom avoid getting caught each time, but it actually suited me far better when all the focus was on him. It meant my day-to-day exploits went unnoticed.

Gramma moved in a little after my sixteenth birthday. As a joke, one of my friends bought me a 'grow your own marijuana' plant. It came in a colourful tie-dye patterned box adorned with the ubiquitous leaf symbol. My friend assured me it was bought from a well-known department store in the city centre. I read the instructions on the box in detail, which told me that the seeds would grow into a plant that looked and smelled like marijuana but actually wasn't. It was a spider plant. Something called cleome, I think. In fact, it had none of the necessary attributes required to make any smoker high.

I must have caught my dad on a good day, because after he'd read and reread the packaging, he agreed that it would be fun for me to grow the plant. I don't know whether he thought tending to the plant may in some way give me, and perhaps Tom, some focus. He mentioned that he had read somewhere that gardening, and especially caring for and tending to plants, was 'good for people'.

I planted the seeds and placed them in a nice sun trap in the conservatory. It only took a week or two for the first seedlings to begin to emerge. They looked like watercress or mustard cress at first, until the little green capsules opened and the familiar five-pointed leaf unfurled. I was overjoyed, amazed that a tiny, dry seed could – with the addition of something as simple as water and light – leave its state of dormancy and become something altogether new.

Something living.

Something tangible.

As the plants grew, we re-potted them into larger pots which filled the windowsills of the conservatory. It was the perfect environment for them, taking near ten hours of south-facing light all day, every day.

Leaf after leaf unfurled, and the plants became a family hobby. My dad would read whatever gardening tips he could, just to ensure that nothing could go wrong with the plants. For once the house was calm. Tom was interested. The arguments ceased. In hindsight, Dad's keen interest obviously revolved less around the plants and more around the fact that our home life was slightly more manageable.

As the plants reached around a foot or so in height, we re-potted them again, and Dad showed us how to tame the branches, forcing them to grow in a circle mirroring the edge of the pot. One afternoon, when Tom noticed that the leaves on one of the plants were yellowing prematurely, the event was treated as a family emergency. We acted as if a family pet were unwell. We paced the house, fed it nutrients, watched it almost around the clock and nursed it back to health. That was the only time that I can remember us all pulling together.

The smell from the conservatory was becoming overwhelming and the door which led into the house had to be kept shut at all times. The fumes were strong, sweet and pungent, and if you breathed in enough, you could persuade yourself that you were feeling the effects. It was nearly three months before the growth stage slowed and the plants began to flower. The buds were large and sticky, and ugly to look at. A sugary coating covered the small leaves which surrounded the flowers like a lion's mane.

We waited patiently until it was time to cut them down and harvest them. The four of us sat around the kitchen table armed with different-sized scissors and secateurs, cutting off each of the buds one by one and dropping them in a large trifle bowl that Gramma had found under the sink. It took us hours. There were nine plants in total, and by the time we had finished we had filled a fruit bowl as well.

For that short time, we were all connected again. I distinctly remembered us all laughing after Dad commented what a field day the police would have if they arrived right now. The explaining that we'd need to do. Wasn't it enough that they were sniffing around anyway, without us having a few grand's worth of 'weed' on the kitchen table?

Gramma hoovered around and threw the stiff stalks and brittle branches away. When she had finished, Dad asked, "What are we actually going to do with this stuff?"

"Smoke it," Gramma said with a wink.

"I think it'd give you a bit of a headache," I said.

There were two huge bowls on the kitchen table filled to the brim with green, heady plant matter. Almost all buds.

"No, seriously," Dad said.

"We'll keep it," I said. "I can trick my mates."

Tom laughed.

"What do you mean?" Dad asked.

"Well, it looks real enough. I can bag it up, and when they come over, I can pretend I have the real thing. Think about Darren's face."

Tom laughed again.

Dad opened his mouth.

A moment too late.

"Plus," I said, "it'd be good to have at home. We know it's not real, but if the police turn up to search again and find it, they'll arrest you for supplying or something and then have to admit later on they made a mistake."

I could see Dad was thinking about this. Gramma sat back down at the table.

"What's happening?" she asked.

Dad explained. I could tell he thought that my idea might have legs. He told Gramma that it would look good if the police were made to seem inept. Gramma nodded. I couldn't tell whether she understood or was just agreeing because Dad seemed so enthusiastic. She pulled out the drawer on her side of the kitchen table and removed a half-filled box of sandwich bags.

The four of us proceeded to fill and seal the bags one by one. We ended up with fourteen in total. Tom and I placed the bags in the bowls and carried one each to the bottom of the stairs.

"Make sure you put some under my bed," Dad called behind us. "Or in my underwear drawer."

"Will do," we said.

As we approached the landing at the top of the stairs, Tom stopped and turned. I was a few steps below.

"Shame it's not real," he whispered, winking.

"Yeah," I said, climbing the top stair to the landing, "shame I switched the seeds with the real thing."

"Fuck off," he said.

I just smiled.

"Seriously?"

I smiled again and watched his eyes buzz around like a meat fly trying to avoid a bright light. He was trying to gauge whether my smile held any truth.

I just waited, and a moment later a huge, beaming grin crossed his face.

Chapter 32

I stretch and yawn, and then feel instant guilt that Gramma may have heard me and could infer that I am bored watching her expire.

I am conscious that I have been alongside her bed for nearly four hours. I am not sure whether this is a long time or not. How long do you wait for someone to die? My immediate answer to myself is: *I suppose you wait until they die.* But that could still be days away and I can't just sit in silence while I wait. Should her final moments be spent in silence?

I feel guilty because I have a vested interest in it all happening very quickly so that *my* life can return to normal. I'll be standing alongside her, stroking her hair, stroking her hand, all feeling very disingenuous, of course, because inside I'll be willing for her next breath to be her last. There is no dignity for her in that. Plus, I don't actually know how close to death she is, and I'm not sure it's a question I want to ask Jacqui, or Tony, or Susan. I mean, come on, how do you phrase a question like that and still make it seem like you are concerned?

Once again, I am annoyed by the fact that I have been left to carry this burden alone.

No one trains you for this.

A little guidance would be nice.

I am therefore relieved when there is a light knock at the door and Jacqui enters.

"Hi," she says, her voice no more than a whisper. I am instantly suspicious that she knows something I don't.

"How is she?" she asks.

Of course, I don't know the answer. She is pretty much as she was. At least I think she is. Four hours ago she was lying here silently, her eyes closed, her breathing slow but regular, her movement near zero. And now when Jacqui asks her question, Gramma is doing exactly the same things. Does this mean she is doing well or not?

I shrug. It's the best I can do.

"I know it can be hard to tell," Jacqui says gently. "Is there anyone else taking over?"

"Taking over?"

"Like other family members. That type of thing?"

"No. There's just me."

"Well, you need to go home and get some rest," she says. "You can't be expected to sit here all day and all night."

"Well…" I say, for no other reason than I want her to continue speaking.

"I know, I know," she says, "you'll feel guilty if you're not here. Do you live far?"

"Fifteen-minute walk."

"Get yourself off then. Get some food, some rest. Come back when you're recharged a bit. We'll be here for her while you're away. Checking up on her."

I have to say I am relieved. It's a strange feeling that I needed the authority of a complete stranger to allow me to leave my guilt at the door.

I pull on my coat.

Jacqui moves in toward me and I can smell the perfume on her skin. Her words are almost breathless and I can feel them on my neck.

"We'll call you if there's any change. Now, get some rest."

Chapter 33

I am back home and logged on just in time for my meeting to open. I am disappointed that there are only six attendees. This increases my chances of having to speak and reduces my ability to hide.

33.30
-1.30

It is clear from the meeting that my strategies for, shall we say, manipulating my daily workload have now been exposed. There are multiple references made (without directly pointing fingers, of course) about actions that staff have been taking to appear to be working. My colleague Brian (whom I have worked alongside electronically for three years) is the whistleblower. He is claiming credit for the discovery of underhanded employee activity, information which I openly gave him and, more to the point, he himself has been using for at least a year. It seems that his recent promotion has made him morally bankrupt and given him the authority to throw me under the corporate bus. It's all very disappointing.

But at this moment in time, it is low on my list of 'very important things I need to deal with'.

I log off and get back on the floor.

I need to find the third witness.

"So, she is actually dying?" Tom says.

"Yeah. She is."

"Like, actually?"

"Like, actually, Tom."

"Okay, man. Yeah, I dunno what to think."

I tell him of Gramma's condition and how she looked earlier that day. He sounds more confused than anything. This is normal for Tom, but he tells me his main struggle is why I am actually bothered. Why I am even visiting her. I find it hard to explain.

"You're being evasive, man," he says. "Tell me again."

"Okay, so, I found out she was dying –"

"How?"

"Doesn't matter, Tom. She's only round the corner from here. It's a small village. People talk."

"Okay."

"I didn't think it was right that she died alone."

"Why?"

"Dunno. Seems like morally the right thing to do is to be with her."

"After all that she's put you, put us, through?"

"I know –"

"Not just that. You're basically doing this as a favour for Dad. You're doing a favour for the person who's caused the most shit in our lives, Sam. And not only that, the person who's caused *the second most shit* is the person you're visiting. What the fuck, man?"

He has a point. I know that. But just because they have acted in that way, doesn't mean that I have to. I tell him. Of course, he has an answer.

"You're just getting walked over again, man. All over again. Fuck 'em, I say."

I hear the click of his lighter and then a deep pull on whatever he is smoking.

"I know," I say again. I can't find the words to express to him why I am doing what I am doing. It is something I am unable to put into words. It is a feeling, deep inside me, that is driving my actions. The decisions I am making are all based on a hunch that what I am doing is the right thing to do. When Tom lays out the truth, I can't deny it. I can't argue that he is wrong, because he isn't. That doesn't stop the feeling driving me on, the nagging whisper that I can't even locate inside of me. I just know it's there.

"So?" he sighs, awaiting a logical answer from me. "I'll ask again, Sam. What the fuck?"

"I dunno," I say. "It just seems like something I have to do. Like I no longer have control."

He pulls in smoke again.

"And Gramma mentioned three witnesses who saw Mum. Not two. Three."

"Jesus, Sam." He sounds exasperated. 'We all know what happened. It's all done. It's finished. Get over it. Think about Mum."

"I am."

"Hmm." He sounds far from convinced.

"I take it you're not coming, Tom?"

"You're the only person I'd come for. Not them."

"So, come for me."

"Fuck. I dunno. I can't deal with this shit again, man."

"Think about it," I say, and then quickly add, "but you haven't got long to think."

The phone goes silent and the home screen appears.

It's dark when I reach St Dymphna's.

I have spent the early hours of the evening unsuccessfully trying to find witness three. I am beginning to wonder whether he or she exists. Usually, I wouldn't give up so easily, but I feel like I've read through these documents a hundred times already. Sara and I reviewed the box time and again. I recognise the names of police officers, witnesses, locations, even car registrations. Once this stuff gets in your mind, it is etched there forever like initials on a tree. I get the feeling that this final attempt will end in disappointment and, unless there is a staggering miracle, Tom and I will never find out about our past. We will be forced to live with the unknown until the day we die.

The door is buzzed open from inside and I push it. Nobody comes to greet me and the office door is, for the first time, closed. I scan the hallway and dining room at the end of the corridor but see no-one. With that, I go straight down to Gramma's room, accompanied by a gnawing feeling which seems to be preparing me for something.

I take a breath and blow it out through circled lips. Then I push open the door and step inside.

The television could not possibly be louder. The volume is up so high, there is a dull buzz at the end of each sentence, which I can only think is the speaker vibrating against the frame of the television. I am surprised to see Gramma sitting up in a much lower bed. The frame has been removed at the end where her feet lie – I suspect so she can see the television, which has been angled toward her.

"Hello, Samuel," she says jauntily. "What a lovely surprise."

I take the remote control and begin to turn the volume down. I am confused. As I slide the high-backed chair across the floor, I check again that I am in the correct room. There is no comparison to how she was earlier in the day. She looks clean, and the colour has returned to her cheeks. I didn't expect her eyes to be open, never mind for her to speak.

"Hi, Gramma," I say. "You look a lot better."

"I feel it," she says. Her eyes roll back and then return to focus on me.

"You don't mind me turning the TV down?"

"No, dear. It's all rubbish. Do you know, there are so few programmes that aren't repeats nowadays, they have to put 'new' in front of the title so you can tell."

I smile, amazed at how lucid she is.

"They used to put a little 'r' in the paper after the programme name, to tell you it was a repeat. Not now. It's all changed. It's all back to front."

"You're right," I say.

"What have you been watching?" I ask.

"Oh, I don't know, Samuel."

The side of the bed is at waist height, but now that I am seated Gramma towers above me, like some Egyptian queen. Me? Her lowly subject.

"Is this a new bed?"

"I don't think so," she says.

"It seems a lot lower."

"It's that thing on the wire," she says, pointing weakly.

I follow the grey wire to a white control box which is hooked on the bottom rung of her cage. I lift it off – an array of stick-men pictures show me that the bed has varying positions and heights. I put the box back.

Gramma takes a sip of water from her tip-cup. She turns her head to face me.

"What does that say?" she asks, looking at my chest.

I look down, then open my hoodie so she can see my t-shirt. It's black, with a small typewriter font across the front.

"Er, it says, 'Coagulation Saved My Life'."

"Why?"

For no reason, I am suddenly embarrassed.

"It's like a joke. A pun."

"Oh," she says, unimpressed. She turns away from me and faces the television again.

Chapter 34

I am asked to leave the room when Jacqui and Tony arrive.

I sit outside in the corridor and contemplate ringing Sara again. I know her well enough to know that if she feels under pressure or cornered, she will push back. She will refuse to help, because she doesn't like how the pressure feels. She will claim that the stress of getting involved is too much. Therefore, I have to tread gently.

It's a shame that we split up.

I can't tell you the exact reason, because I don't know it. All I know is that when we reached the point that Sara moved out, there was no argument. There was no screaming. No finger-pointing. No blame. And there was certainly no chance that one of us was going to beg the other not to give up. This wasn't like a piece of a jigsaw was missing. It was more that neither of us could believe we even began the puzzle in the first place.

Our relationship was based on a pathological obsession about finding my mother. My obsession was, of course, based on deep-rooted emotions: loss, rejection, anxiety, depression, despair. Sara was altogether more disconnected. Her obsession was based on solving a mystery, righting an injustice and probably, in all honesty, looking good for her future legal career. Mix these conflicting emotions and motives together – along with the voice of logic and reason – and you've created the saltiest of broths. Toward the end, when emotions were running increasingly high, the broth boiled. And if there was ever a chance of saving our relationship... well, it had gone.

During this period, Sara inadvertently became my mother figure. This was purely accidental; however, it could have been predicted from the start. It doesn't take a genius to work out that if somebody has rejection issues caused by the absence of a mother figure, then it is likely they will cling to the first surrogate who appears. For Sara, well at first anyway, our initial meetings were strictly business. She wanted to solve a mystery. But I truly believe that she fell in love with me or maybe us quite near the beginning. At the time when the conversation never fell silent. During the late nights when we poured through documents, seeking the truth. When everything was exciting. It's far more likely that she fell in love with what we represented as a whole rather than the individual components.

We spent years trying to force pieces of the puzzle into places where the pieces weren't supposed to go. We tried to match spaces to pieces and pieces to spaces, and where one didn't quite fit, we'd pretend that it did. It was only at the end that we realised we were trying to create a picture from two incomplete and non-matching jigsaw sets.

An impossible picture.

I idly finger my phone and decide to leave it to Sara to call me back in her own time. I know that solving my mother's disappearance means far too much to her for her to wait too long.

Jacqui leaves the room first. She seems to be in a hurry, her eyes fixed on what I assume is a message on her phone. Tony comes out a moment later.

"Mr Samuel," he says, "how are you today?"

"Fine, thanks, Tony. You?"

"Oh, busy. Not too many staff. But many residents."

I nod.

"Mrs Joan is good this afternoon. Clean sheets. Clean pillows. Nice for her."

"I know. Earlier, I thought that it might be the end. But now..."

"Yes, she looks much better."

I have to be careful phrasing my next question. I am sure that it has been asked of Tony numerous times before, perhaps with one eye on the enormous daily costs of the home and the legacies payable under the Will. This, of course, doesn't concern me. It's time that I need. So does Gramma, for that matter.

"How long do you think Gramma has? It's just –"

He shakes his head. "I don't know. Could be...I don't know. I don't."

I want to push him, to get a precise answer. Maybe it's my nature, but just a clue would be nice. Anything between an hour and a week would be helpful. But then I realise that Tony doesn't have any idea. He may be around people in the late stages of their lives day in, day out, but sometimes people who appear perfectly healthy die completely out of the blue. They are smiling and laughing and eating, and then the next morning they are stiff and cold. Other times, people get cancer or have heart attacks in their eighties and still live another ten years. Based on earlier, I expect Tony would have told me that Gramma had no more than twenty-four hours. The way she appears now, you could expect her to live another year. I decide it isn't fair to pressure him further.

He simply doesn't know.

Nobody does.

Not even Gramma, and it's her death we are talking about.

"Can you turn this rubbish off, Samuel?"

I get up from the armchair and switch off the television.

"I don't like it at this time," she says. "It's all stupid people."

It's just past nine. The watershed. We've spent a good proportion of my time there today part-

watching television and part-chatting. In fact, the largest part has been the television watching. Gramma has seemed content to stare down the length of her bed, turning to me only once or twice in the last few hours. Perhaps to see if I was still there.

She yawns and tells me that she is getting tired. Could I close the curtains? Could I pull her covers over her? Could I move her cuddly animals to where she can see them?

I switch her lamp on and turn off the main light. She turns to me and I stroke her hand with my thumb.

"Gramma? There's something I have to ask," I say quietly. I don't wait for her to reply. "The other day you mentioned three people saw Mum after she disappeared."

She smiles weakly and there is a vague hint of a nod.

"Are you sure there were three? Because in the box, y'know the papers, I can only find two."

"There were three," she croaks.

"Are you sure?"

She turns her hand and links it with mine. She gives me a light squeeze.

"There were three, Samuel."

She closes her eyes and whispers, "Will Thomas come?"

Less than a minute later, her breathing is more audible. She sucks it in through her nose and pushes it out through pursed lips. I continue to stroke her hand, watching the ripples of skin gather before I smooth them out with my thumb.

When I am sure she is asleep, I quietly get up from the chair and kiss her on the forehead. I hope that her eyes are open again in the morning.

As I leave, I notice Tony is sitting at the desk just inside the office door. He seems to be inputting information onto a spreadsheet.

"Good night, Mr Samuel," he says.

"Good night, Tony."

I hear the buzzer signal that I can leave and pull the handle to open the door. Then I close it again. I go back to the open office door.

"Er, Tony?"

He jumps slightly and spins his chair to face me. He pats his heart.

"Mr Samuel," he says, "I'm sorry. I thought you had, er, left, er, gone. Home."

"Sorry, I didn't mean to startle you," I say, instantly wondering whether he's understood my sentence.

"S'okay. I think you have gone. I think you go through door. Outside. Home."

He breathes out a long breath. He seems relieved.

I apologise again. "Tony, you know the other day, I lost my jacket? My coat?"

"Yes. Yes."

He stares at me warily, probably confused that I am wearing the 'lost' coat.

"In the pocket was my wallet."

He squints through almost closed eyes.

"My money."

"Aah, okay," he smiles.

"When I got the coat back, my money was gone."

"Gone?"

"Gone. Missing. Not there anymore."

"Your money was gone?"

"From the jacket."

"Oh." He sounds surprised. "The money gone from your coat?"

"Yes."

"Okay. I write down. I speak to Susan. She had your coat."

He spins back around and scribbles a note on a scrappy-looking foolscap pad. From here, I can't make out his spidery writing. In fact, I can't tell whether it is even in English.

He turns back to me.

"I ask," he says, "I ask Susan. Tomorrow."

"Okay, thanks," I say, unable to get any clues from his face.

Behind him, his shiny coat is neatly on a hanger hooked over the side of a filing cabinet.

Chapter 35

The evening is unusually warm and I leave my jacket unfastened for the walk home. I unzip my jacket pocket and pull out my phone. I turn off flight mode and wait to catch up with what may or may not have happened in the last three or so hours.

I have a couple of texts from friends. Jonathan starts a new job tomorrow. Kellie is bitching about not being able to find a job that fits around her childcare. Darren has sent me pictures of enormous tits, as usual. I am beginning to wonder just how many hours a day he spends searching for a bigger pair to outdo the previous image.

I also have two missed calls. Both from Sara. There is one voicemail, which was left after the first call. She asks me to ring her back when I have five minutes. There is no message with the second call. I suspect that she doesn't want me to know just how desperate she is to hear from me. I lived with her for years. I know exactly how desperate she is. As easy to read as a children's picture book.

I call her back whilst I walk. She answers on the first ring, which does nothing to disguise her desperation.

"Hey, Sam," she says. She is far more upbeat than earlier in the day. "You okay?"

"Yeah, good, thanks. You?"

"Better now," she says, "long day. Look, sorry about this morning. It was early."

"I get it. No need to apologise."

"How's your gramma?"

"She's dying, Sara. I thought earlier today, but now she's brightened again."

It suddenly strikes me that Sara has never met my gramma.

She fell into the time period after my relationship with Gramma was reduced to ashes. She has now reappeared when Gramma will quite literally go the same way soon.

"How come you're seeing her? I thought..."

"I know. So did I. But I'm the only one who can visit. And –"

"You hoped you might find out something? Before it's too late?"

It seems I am as easy to read as Sara is.

"I suppose so, yeah."

"And what have you found?"

"Well, Gramma says that there were three witnesses who saw Mum in the week after she disappeared. Before this week, it's always been two. Not three."

"I know," she says, and I suddenly realise that I am speaking to someone who probably has more knowledge of the case than me. "That's weird. Is she sure?"

"There's nothing in the papers about a third witness –"

"Sam, I know."

"Yeah, sorry, sure. I don't know whether it's just her memory or the drugs she's on or whatever, but she seems resolute."

"Have you asked her who they are?"

"Who?"

"The witnesses. What their names are?"

She doesn't try to hide the tinge of frustration that has crept into her voice.

"No. Not as such. She's too old. I can't interrogate her. But she's said it more than once. On different days."

There is a silence while Sara considers what I have said.

"Plus," I add, "she's too old to remember names. *I'd* be hard pushed to remember without having the papers to look through."

"Jocelyn Brooks. Annabel Hunt."

"Yeah, okay, I get it," I say, secretly pleased that someone with Sara's knowledge now seems to be completely onside.

"Sorry to ask, Sam, but how long has she got?"

"I don't know. Like I said, I thought she was going to die earlier today."

"Listen," she says, "we need to know. You need to know. You have to ask her."

"I've asked her twice, and twice she's confirmed that there are three witnesses. She told me it was in the papers."

"And is it? No, it's not, of course it's not in there. We've been through it a thousand times."

"Make it a thousand and one. I'm going through it all again."

"And?"

"Nothing."

"So..."

"That's why I called you. I don't know what to do next."

"I'll come over. We'll have one last look."

"Seriously?"

"Yeah. I can do Sunday."

"Great."

"I'll text you a time."

"No worries."

And she's gone.

I open the front door and immediately kick off my shoes. They land almost perfectly alongside one another on the rug. I smile and turn the key to lock the door. Instantly, I hear sounds coming from behind the almost-closed kitchen door. I stand with my back against the wall which separates the hall from the kitchen. I am a few inches from the door frame.

I slow my breathing and listen.

I hear drawers open and close, accompanied by the sound of cutlery meeting cutlery and plates being returned to their home. Above the clinking of crockery and the metallic clang of pans being dried and put away, I can hear her voice. I don't recognise the song, but the melody is slow and has an almost ethereal quality. Near hymn-like. Mum sings in a high-pitched, sweet-as-sugar voice which reminds me of Enya or The Sundays or Sixpence None the Richer. The type of voice that is so sweet you'd expect to put on weight just listening to it. I can tell from the way she is singing that she is smiling. It's strange that you can know somebody so well that you can tell simply from their voice how they look at that moment.

I imagine that Mum takes a plate from the draining rack next to the sink and dries it with a tea towel whilst she spins and twirls in the direction of the cupboard she will place it in. I imagine that she uses the tea towel as a prop, stretching it out and lifting it excitedly above her head. I imagine that she skips and dances from one side of the kitchen to the other. Smiling, always smiling. Mum always had a way of finding some joy in everything she attempted. If there was none in her marriage, then she'd find it in other places.

I am desperate to move from the safety of the wall into the door frame, to see her whilst she cleans. To see her smile. To watch her mouth form the words of the song. To watch her move. For one last time.

But I know that I won't move. I don't have the courage. Though I can't see her, for all intents and purposes she is in the room next door to me. We are separated only by a matter of feet. I can hear her, but I can't move my feet to see her. I can't take the risk of showing myself to her. Because I don't know what I'd do if when I looked she wasn't there. Whilst I can hear her, she is there. She is living, breathing and singing and almost within reach.

I'd rather stay where I am and listen.

Chapter 36

35.00
-0.00

It's near midnight by the time I log off MySnug. I was grateful to see both numbers turn from red to green – the signal that I have completed my working hours for the week. It's always a relief to reach this milestone, though it's usually Sunday afternoon when I finally finish my hours. I'm two days ahead this week and perhaps I'll enjoy the feeling a little better.

On a usual week, the numbers would turn green for a matter of hours, then I'd log in again on Monday morning and they'd be that angry shade of red again. The red gives me the feeling that someone somewhere is annoyed with me and will stay that way until I turn their numbers a more acceptable colour. Green. The universal language of go. Go be free. Go be unshackled from your working week. I toss the mouse across the desk and stretch back in the chair.

I can't believe that my week comprises watching numbers count down at the same rate that my life slips away. That I am only ever happy when I have managed to turn the figures green. By definition this means that I am unhappy the vast majority of the time, because the numbers reset every single Monday at eight a.m. precisely.

Every week.
Every month.
Every year.
This is my existence.
Literally.
This.
Is.
It.
Something has to change.

I think I hear my phone ringing. At first I am unsure where the sound is coming from. It is a distant chime, like an unexpected church bell, its sound suffocated by the dense fog of my dreams.

I ignore the phone and lie on my back, trying to make sense of the experience that I've just had. The place I have just visited in my dream seemed very much like my day-to-day reality. The rooms were the same. The faces were the same. The outside world was the same. But the space had been filled with a golden sepia hue. It is hard to describe. It was almost as if you were looking at my everyday life through a pane of glass that had been painted. My life was still visible on the other side, it was just coloured incorrectly. I am reminded of the plastic screens that used to be attached to the inside of shop windows to stop the products within fading, the screens that made everything behind them appear the same golden yellow colour. In the same way that snow covers everything in the crisp cleanliness of white.

This is the main indication that what I just experienced didn't happen. If the colours had been natural, I would still be questioning if it actually happened, struggling with that feeling when you wake and for a moment you cannot work out the difference between external and inner reality.

I notice that I am out of breath. Instead of sleeping in my bed, I was running. My experience was so vivid that although I haven't run anywhere, my mind believes that I have. I need air to fill my lungs.

In the dream, Gramma and Tom and Dad were sitting at a table outside on the patio. They were animated, but I was too far away to hear what they were saying. My dream told me that whatever they were talking about was negative. They were arguing about something. I was running at full speed down the side of the house to get to them, but I wasn't moving. I was trapped behind an invisible curtain which stretched as I ran and trapped me within it, my hands, my face, my features moulded in the transparent, stretched blanket.

In my hand I held my phone. I had to tell them what had happened. I knew that as soon they heard, whatever they were discussing would be irrelevant. Their lives were to instantly become entirely different. I remember the feeling of power knowing that what I was about to say was going to change the direction of the rest of their lives. I now realised that all along I had been holding back a secret. Everything in the world had changed. And if it was to have a bonfire-toffee hue to it, then so be it.

I tried to attract their attention as I ran, but my words were deflected back at me. My shouts bounced back from the curtain, amplified. It was clear my calls were inaudible to them. The sounds were piercing, like the calls of a crow, and I stopped running and sank to my knees. When the sound waves stopped deflecting, all was quiet.

I was left on my knees waving the phone, waving my hands, trying to attract their attention. Dad was facing me, yet he couldn't see me. I had the distinct feeling that as he glanced at the lawn down the side of the house all he could see was what he expected to see. Green grass. Green plants. Blue sky.

I dropped my phone and continued to wave my arms in silence until they tired. Then – still unnoticed – I collapsed to the damp pecan-coloured grass beneath me.

It is the repeated ringing of the phone that brings my mind back to the here and now.

Each time I ignore the ringing, it becomes louder, as if my journey to reality is nearing an end. The room is charcoal black and for a moment I can't tell what colour world I am in. I am now acutely aware of being in bed. I can feel the cotton gripped in my hands, the warmth of the duvet. I am confused by the lack of light. There is always light in here. I rub my eyes and push my fringe from my forehead. It stays where I push it, trained by the sweat that drips from each hair.

I can make out the familiar shapes of my wardrobe and television in the darkness and I am convinced I am at home. I hear the phone ring yet again, and for the first time I turn to face it. It is exactly where I expected it to be, face down on the bedside table. On each ring, light escapes around the edges of the screen, forming a dull halo. Then it becomes invisible again for a moment before the border of light returns.

I turn the phone. It's four fifteen in the morning. I have seventeen missed calls. Before I get the chance to return the call, Tom rings again.

I rub my eyes. "Tom."

"At fucking last," he says, slurring. I can tell that he too is not in this world, but for different reasons.

"It's fucking four in the morning."

"I know, man. I know. I know. I know it is." His words crash into one another like cars in a pile-up. I can't tell where one begins and the next ends.

"What's up?"

I'm ready to hear his story of the evening he has just spent with Freddie Mercury and Jim Morrison, no doubt shooting up at the Viper Room on Sunset Boulevard or something similar.

"I'm gonna come," he says, "I'm gonna come up. Come see you. See you. See Gramma."

"Yeah?"

"Yeah. For you, though, Sam. That's the only reason, man. Yeah? You get me?"

"Yeah. That's good, Tom."

"For you, man. It's all for you."

In my imagination, I can see his clenched fist beating against his heart as he speaks.

"That's good."

"Yeah. Yeah. Yeah, it is." He sounds like he is already questioning his choice; his words seem to spill from his mouth more quickly than his brain can attach meaning to them.

"You sure that's –"

"Yeah. Yeah. I'm sure. I'm sure. I'm gonna come. For you, though, man. For you, 'cos you're my brother, y'know. D'ya know what I mean?"

"Okay."

There is a high chance that he won't remember this call. I can hear voices and music in the background.

"Yeah, man. I'm coming up. Look, I gotta go, okay?"

"When?"

"What?"

"When, Tom?"

"When what?"

"When are you coming up?"

"Oh, yeah. Er, I dunno. Next week probably. Yeah?"

"I don't think that'll be soon enough, Tom."

"Okay. Listen, I gotta go. I'll be up. Like, maybe tomorrow or something?"

I lie on my back and consider the chances of Tom returning to the house that holds all the memories he has spent twenty years trying to blank out or chemically destroy.

I appreciate his call, but I don't expect to see him.

Chapter 37

I sleep until well after lunchtime and wake feeling refreshed.

Spectacularly bright sunlight streams in through the windows, which gives a gentle warmth to the house. It makes it feel like the house is suddenly awakening from a deep slumber. Like it wants to be lived in again.

The sunlight exposes dust on every surface, and I spend the next few hours cleaning accompanied by the Manic Street Preachers. I laugh to myself, remembering their bassist wearing a t-shirt sporting the words: 'I ♥ hoovering'. I wonder whether I subconsciously chose the music with this in mind. I also wonder whether my unplanned cleaning spree is related to the arrival of Sara tomorrow. To show her that I'm surviving here. That I'm on top of things. That I'm strong and I've dealt with everything my past threw at me.

I don't know.

I don't understand much of what is being processed in my mind right now.

I don't understand much of anything.

You'll have to forgive me.

It's a lot to take in.

I make it to the top of the drive of St Dymphna's at around five.

Susan greets me at the door.

"She's not very good, I'm afraid."

This doesn't seem like the time to ask Susan about my missing property.

"Oh?" I say.

"Yes, she's been bad through the night again. We've been monitoring her. You can go through. I just wanted to warn you."

I push open the door to find a room oblivious to the striking sunlight outside. A thin parallelogram of light is thrown across the carpet from where the curtain has become unhooked, but that aside, the room is dark. I can just make out Gramma's shape on the bed. The sheets are pushed to her feet, where I notice the cage has been reattached.

I open the curtains a little further, widening the shape cast by the sun. I pull over the chair and lower the bed so we are at the same level. I can see the back of her head, and in some ways I am pleased that she is not facing me. I don't think I would wish to be staring directly at her as the final moments of her life play out. I'm not sure she'd like it either.

Once again, I feel out of my depth. Aside from her breathing, the room is soundless and my brain quickly trains itself to the rhythmic routine of the air.

I want to wake her. To bring her back. To ask her one more time. I don't want her to die with her secrets.

I feel trapped.

I feel lost inside my own life.

I want to open my mouth and speak, but the silence in the room makes every attempt to do so seem trite. Is there any point in speaking when no-one can hear? I want to unload my past onto her and remove it from myself. I wonder if speaking my thoughts will physically pass them to her and she can take them over to the other side with her. She can carry the burden wherever her afterlife may be and it will no longer be something I have to bear. If there is no afterlife – and I strongly suspect there isn't – then she can still carry my words into whatever kind of nothingness is waiting for her.

Suddenly, she jerks and her body twists. Her head faces toward me, her mouth open, saliva connecting her mouth to the pillow like a spider's thread. A gravelly sound comes from somewhere deep in her throat. It's guttural, a cross between a grunt and a groan. She is trying to speak. She lifts her naked arm ever so slightly and I see her index finger curl outwards.

I stand. Only because it seems like the correct thing to do. I feel like I am ready for action if I am on my feet. God only knows what I am supposed to do next.

The gravelly sound comes again. It's a deep, knotted breath mixed with mucus and whatever else is coming from her chest. The sound cracks and splits as she pushes it through her mouth. Her finger unfurls again.

I place my hand on her arm. It's cold to touch.

Her eyes open slightly and some of the crust from her tear duct crumbles away and floats lightly onto her cheek. She pushes the noise out again. This time louder. It may just be me, but her eyes seem to be pleading with me. Begging me. I don't know what to do.

Is she thirsty? Hungry? In pain? Cold?

I am annoyed. I should know what to do. I should be able to help her. I am reminded of when Tom was a baby and would cry for hours. The frustration of Mum as she fed him, tried to get him to sleep, made him comfortable, gave him his dummy (again). Nothing worked. 'If only he could tell me what was wrong,' she used to say to me, wiping away the tears from her own face.

Gramma makes the guttural noise again and I realise I am just going to have to guess. I pick up her tip-cup and hold it in front of her water-logged eyes. I don't even know if she can see.

"Water?" I whisper. It feels strange to hear my own voice break the near-silence. "Gramma? Do you want water? Are you thirsty?"

She makes the sound again. It's nothing more than a grunt, but it sounds different, somehow more urgent. I put the water down.

I stroke her arm. Goosebumps appear instantly, and I try to warm her with my hand in an attempt to smooth them down.

"What is it?" I whisper. "What can I do to help you?"

Grrnt.

"Are you in pain?"

Grrnt.

And then, suddenly, it's obvious.

I collect the sheets from her feet and shake them out slightly, before pulling them up and over the thin grey skin that covers what is left of her shoulders.

She closes her eyes and I am sure I can see the smallest hint of a smile.

Chapter 38

As you would expect, my teenage years, the years after Mum vanished, were the very worst of my life.

It only got worse after Gramma moved in.

When Mum first disappeared, the police were almost permanently camped at our house. Initially, they treated the matter as a simple disappearance. But whatever information it was that they received over the next week, it changed the direction of the investigation and there was no reversing that. There is nothing in those police papers that suggests why the focus changed to my father, but clearly it did. And once they had him in their sights, they were inextricably blinkered to the extent that they could no longer see anything else.

They stayed for days on end, digging up parts of the garden, searching inch by inch inside and outside the house. They took my father's car. They took his clothes. They took anything that 'could be relevant'.

Once their initial searches and burrowing into the sticky clay ground outside returned no results – nothing – they moved into more of a mental torture stage. They would appear at all times, night or day, just for a few moments with Dad. A few questions, that's all.

Grind him down.

Interrupt his sleep.

Keep him on edge.

Tire him.

Confuse him.

Break him.

At the time, it hadn't even crossed my mind that Dad may even be a suspect. Why weren't they finding Mum? Where was she?

The daily visits continued. The police asked the same questions over and over and over again. Looking for a hint of inconsistency in his story. Finding the smallest of holes to pick at. And just like a woollen sweater, the more they picked and pushed their fingers through, the larger the hole would become. The most minute of historic incidents or pieces of 'evidence' were suddenly given enormous weight. Time passes, memories change, memories fade.

And then one day they didn't come.

Nor the next.

There were rumours that the police were chasing up other leads, though we were never clear exactly what they were and there is nothing in the box that suggests that these mysterious leads were ever recorded. There is a statement by a police officer about someone fitting my mum's description turning up at a police station hundreds of miles from home to confirm that her family shouldn't worry; she was very much alive. Apparently, my mum simply walked into a local station and told the police her name and that people were looking for her. "Look," she said, "here I am. I'm alive and well."

She told the officer that she had even left a note to say she was leaving. She was 'at pains' to make the officer understand that the purpose of her visit was to put her family's mind at rest. She was 'fine'.

The policeman recorded this, and our local constabulary were notified. A copy of his statement found its way into the files. The problem was that he hadn't thought to ask 'Mum' for any identification. He hadn't even noted how he knew that she matched Mum's description when at that stage he had never heard of my mother and therefore wouldn't have had anything to compare her with. This event seemed to put back the local investigation by a month or two. The police stopped visiting our home, they stopped hassling Dad, they just stopped.

And then out of the blue (if you'll pardon the pun) they began arriving at the house again. With the benefit of the files, it is clear that a report – from one of their own, no less – about the missing woman appearing wasn't good enough. It didn't fit with their narrative that Dad had killed her and dumped her somewhere. They *knew* that he had something to do with it and they were determined to find out how he near carried out the perfect crime. If I had a penny for each time I heard them tell me or my gramma or my father that they were 'just doing their job', I'd be the proud owner of a gold pig by now.

It was about this time that Gramma came to stay permanently. My father spent the evenings sipping bourbon and the days pacing from room to room. Wherever he was, Tom and I made sure we weren't. Our house had never been a place of calm and in the current situation we were both genuinely scared. Scared of what he may do. To himself or to us. He was careering toward breaking point and the strategic interruptions in his everyday life were beginning to take their toll.

Gramma decided she would sell her house and the money would be used to subsidise us all. My father could no longer work, and there was no money coming in. It all made sense. In addition, Gramma could try to reduce the pressure on my father: caring for Tom and me, cooking, cleaning, baking, whatever.

When the police arrived, Gramma would take us into a different room and keep guard over us. It was certainly us and them by now. The last thing that Dad needed was the police trying to make a case by turning me or Tom against him.

But that is what happened.

Exactly what happened.

Chapter 39

There were two detectives, whose names, if you care to google my mother's disappearance, you can find very easily. For the purposes of what I am about to tell you, I won't name them. It's a public record. It adds nothing for me stir up their names again, put them back in the limelight. I'm not scared of naming them per se, it's just that I know what they are capable of.

The two came as a pair, always a pair. At first, they would simply drive past when I was out walking through the village toward college. Or their car would just appear when I was out with my friends, slowing as it passed. Tall always drove. Red-Face would nod at me from the passenger seat, to let me know he was there. That he could see me.

One day, they pulled in alongside me and a couple of my friends. We were sitting on a stone wall that led over to the back fields, near the woodland. We didn't react quickly enough, and by the time they got out of the car and approached us it would have been far too obvious to throw away the joint we were sharing. I was still holding it when they made the few steps from the car.

"Don't worry," Tall said, nodding to my hand, "we're not interested in that."

I scraped the end of the joint against the wall to put it out and climbed down.

"We could do with a word, Sam," Red-Face said.

"In private. Lads, if you don't mind?" said Tall to my friends.

I nodded.

My friends climbed down from the wall and told me they'd catch up with me later. We waited until they were out of earshot. Now it was just me, Tall and Red-Face.

"So, Sam. We need help," Tall began.

"Okay."

"There's no doubt that your dad killed your mum. Sorry to be so blunt. But it's true. We need your help in proving that," Red-Face said.

"How do you mean?"

"Well, at some stage that morning your dad killed your mum, drove her somewhere and dumped her. That's what we know. What we don't know is where she is," said Tall.

"How do you know he did that?"

"We just know," said Red-Face. "It's a fact. We just need to prove it."

"*How* do you know?"

"All the evidence points to it. Their bad relationship. Your mother wanting to leave him.

The note. The fact that there has been no sign of her for months. The car being cleaned. The digging. It's all there, son," added Tall.

"Dad wouldn't do that," I said. The words sounded empty as they left my mouth, like a box of chocolates where the packaging is intact and when you slide out the tray all the spaces are empty. There is nothing of substance left.

"Wouldn't he?" asked Red-Face. "You're absolutely sure, Sam?"

And the truth was that I wasn't. How could I be sure? I found it hard to believe that Dad had anything to do with it. But then again, it wasn't impossible. Dad was probably capable of anything on the wrong day. That Saturday could easily have been the wrong day.

As could many others.

Tall saw my hesitation and his chance arrive at the same time. "So, will you help us, Sam?"

"By doing what?"

Red-Face seemed pleased with my answer. "Just watching, for now. Looking out for things for us."

Tall added, "You wouldn't want someone to get away with murdering your mum, would you?"

It was the perfect line. I mean, who would answer yes to this question?

"No," I said, frowning. I don't know whether I was angry that I was even asked the question or that I was playing a role in my own manipulation.

"Good," said Tall. He looked at Red-Face.

"Right, we'll get going," Red-Face said, smiling. "Take care, Sam."

"You can finish your spliff now, son," Tall said as he opened the driver's door.

Red-Face waved as the car pulled away.

I relit the joint and sat back on the wall.

Chapter 40

My phone continues to buzz in my pocket for a matter of hours before I feel that I can take it out and actually look at the screen. There is something entirely inappropriate about scrolling through messages and missed calls whilst Gramma lies inches away waiting for her life to be over.

I wait until I think she is asleep, though it is difficult to tell. My only gauge is listening for a change in her breathing. The long inhalations continue, but the exhalations have now been replaced by a quiet lowercase 'p' sound – the pronunciation of the letter by a small child.

"Puh."

Long breath in.

Hold.

Push back out.

"Puh."

Breath. Hold. Push.

"Puh."

Breath. Hold. Push.

"Puh."

From time to time she moves position, and I can

see the 'puh' sound being formed between her top lip and her gums, where her dentures used to be. I stroke her arm and gently repeat the word 'sleep' over and over and over. I want her to be comfortable in these final moments. I want her to close her eyes permanently and for it all to be over for her.

And then, suddenly, I realise that these may be the final words she ever hears. I am conscious that if they are, I am gently encouraging her to die. She can probably hear me telling her to sleep, which is simply a metaphor for me instructing her to die.

The stroking and coaxing now seem wholly inappropriate. Like I am an accessory to her death. Like I am beckoning her to her fate. I stop instantly. I don't know what to do. In the end, I pull out my phone for inspiration.

My phone tells me that Sara has tried to call. As has Tom, multiple times. As has my father, twice. Nobody has left a voicemail, but Tom has sent a message, which asks me simply to ring him.

I watch Gramma for ten minutes more and then excuse myself with a whisper, saying that I'll be back soon.

I head back down the corridor (where I can be comfortable that Gramma won't hear me) and take a seat on one of the chairs-that-don't-look-like-they-were-made-for-sitting-on near the visitors' book.

I call Tom back.

"Hey, man," he answers. "You okay?"

"Yeah, good. You?"

"Yeah. Listen, Sam, I'm on the train tomorrow. Dinner time."

"Dinner time arrive or dinner time leave?"

"Dinner time leave. I'll be with you about three."

"'Kay. I'm at the home now."

"How is she?"

"Not good. She's not talking. She's comfortable, though."

"Right." I hear him breathe in smoke. "How long do you think?"

"I don't know, Tom. No idea."

"I'll be there tomorrow."

I hang up and stretch my legs out in front of me, kneading my legs from thigh to knee. I then curve the base of my spine so it's as concave as possible. I get a slight twinge, which makes me straighten up instantly. I rub the vertebrae where the rogue nerve seems to be hiding.

I stand just as the double doors behind me open. They lead to a part of the home that I've yet to visit. I see the back of Susan first, then the bed, then Jacqui guiding it. Jacqui smiles as I move onto my tiptoes, my back against the wall, so she can pass. As Jacqui manoeuvres the bed past me, I see the occupant of the bed for longer than I would like.

Her hair suggests she is female. The tumbleweed of thin, grey hair surrounds a face that no longer looks worldly. Her skin is Bible-paper thin and I can actually see blood moving around her veins and capillaries beneath where her cheeks were.

Her eyes have sunken, immersed deep in her head, leaving each eye ringed by a greyish-green rim.

Her mouth hangs open like a thirsty dog's, her gums exposed. I follow her neck, and I can see the shape of her windpipe, the cartilage ringed and easily recognisable. As she passes, I see it widen slightly where an old scar runs horizontally across her throat. The scar still looks red, and slightly angry.

The rest of her body is covered by a sheet. I am pleased that I can't see it. Its shape alone is enough to give me nightmares. It looks far too thin to hold a human skeleton. An emaciated nothingness, empty of anything but a pulse.

They push the bed past me and I watch as it is moved into the already emptied room three. The door closes behind them. I expect it will be open again in a few hours. The bed will be vacant but made, the floor clean and shining. The room waiting for its next meal.

I sit with Gramma until the early hours.

My mind races with things I want to say. I know that the time for questions is over. There will be no improvement from this stage. Gramma is not going to suddenly rally.

I want to tell her how the decisions that she made have ostensibly ruined the rest of my life. I want to tell her that her stubbornness and disregard of fact has moulded my whole future. That her ridiculous standpoint regarding my mother has made it impossible for me to move on in life. That her rigidity and refusal to accept my father's guilt have destroyed a family that was already under heavy fire.

But are these the kind of things you leave in the mind of the soon-to-be-deceased? I expect not. Without saying them, though, I am left with that burden.

A burden that is now becoming too heavy to carry.

I leave St Dymphna's at just after two a.m.

It's unusually warm, and the moonlight splashes black silhouettes along the pavement where I walk.

Chapter 41

"Sam?"

I can hear his voice, and I move the phone so it is less muffled by the duvet.

"Sam? Sam?"

My mouth feels dry, my tongue seemingly glued to my palate. I reach for a half-empty can of Coke on my bedside table. It has lost its fizz but helps me to unstick my tongue. I swill the liquid in my mouth and then swallow. That's better.

"Sam? Where the fuck are you?"

I put him on speaker so I can hear him more clearly. I don't have the energy to lift my phone. I'm just too tired.

"I'm here."

"Sam? That you?"

"Dad, I'm here," I bark back, annoyed. I no longer care how I speak to him. It won't change anything now. "Anyway, what's up? What time is it?"

My response seems to catch him off-guard. His voice is quieter, less aggressive. "Er, it's seven. They moved me, so I've not been able to phone."

"Right. So why are you calling at this time?"

"First chance I got. How's Gramma?"

"Not good." *No thanks to you.*

"Shit."

Yeah, I'm sure your current circumstances – your living arrangements for the fifteen years or so – haven't helped things along, have they? I'm sure that they've not added to Gramma's worries at all.

"Yeah. I was there till past two this morning." *Filling in for you, Dad. Y'know, taking on the role that you're supposed to be playing.*

"Sorry, Sam. You know I'd be there if I could."

Hmm.

And at this moment, I don't know whether he would be there or not. Perhaps he should have thought about that when my mum went missing. It is his actions that have brought him here. Brought *us* here. It is wholly down to him that I am now playing surrogate son to his dying mother. He has done this. His selfish choices have led us to this moment. I don't know how I am managing to keep my rage in.

"Sam?"

I can't think of anything else to say, and I get the feeling that this will be the last time I ever speak to him. It is time for me to rid myself of him, remove the leech that has fed on me for too long. I know that although he cannot get to me physically, he is always standing a step behind me wherever I go in life. A shadow. A ghost.

I'm finished.

"Sam? Sam?"

I listen and – for a moment – enjoy the desperation in his voice.

"Sam, where the fuck are you?"

I hear his voice raise into a shout.

"Sam, speak to me for fuck's sake...Sam. I swear to fucking God..."

Then I hear the sound of the receiver crashing into its cradle. Over and over. And, eventually, the line goes dead.

Chapter 42

By force of habit, I log on to MySnug.

It's Sunday morning, and therefore the counters have not yet been reset. They continue to show me that I have no further hours to work this week. There are forty-eight emails to deal with, and I scroll through them, looking for anything that may leap out as important. There are a few meeting requests, which I accept, and a number of compliance emails which are circulated to let us all know that somebody is watching us. They tell us of security breaches, issues and problems found on individual computers and update us about the types of things that they will focus on clamping down on in the following month. However well phrased the emails are, the flowery, let-the-company-put-its-arm-around-you-and-give-you-a-much-needed-hug language doesn't hide the unmistakable underlying threat. They tell us when they have found employees who are not working 'to protocol'. They also tell the rest of us that if we are planning on circumnavigating the system in any way, we will be caught. The all-seeing eye, no less.

There is nothing that immediately needs attending to, and an hour later everything is cleared (for this, read deleted). I am disappointed that I have worked an extra hour for nothing, but I feel better for starting Monday afresh. My phone beeps, and Sara's message tells me that she will be arriving around half past ten.

I am suddenly nervous about her arrival. It's strange that a simple message is enough to change the brain's function. My mind was following a certain path this morning, merrily wandering along a linear line to whatever I had to deal with next. As soon as the message landed, my brain slowed and my thought process directionally shifted. My thoughts are now heading off at a right angle to where, seconds earlier, they were going.

Random thoughts are now jumping like kernels of corn over heat. They pop and explode inside my head like fireworks on New Year's Eve. Some of them are relevant, some of them are memories, others I don't know whether they happened or not. They come at ten a second, and therefore even if I wanted to record what they all were, I wouldn't be capable. It seems that, bizarrely, I do not have the capacity to keep up with my own thoughts.

My brain is taking me along a track that I do not wish to travel. I remember the time Sara and I spent together, the way she looks, the way she smells, her mouth, her words, her kisses, how it feels to hold her. I find myself pacing from room to room with no aim. I find myself staring out of the window, my thoughts somewhere far behind the blinding rays from the sun.

And then my pacing eventually takes me to the stairs, where I find a step to sit on after the turn to the top. I am on the third step, staring over the back garden, over the huge mound of earth. And I am back at our wedding, and I am back at the dreams of the future that I sketched out for Sara and me. I have returned to how beautiful she looked that day, and how in that moment I felt like everything had fallen into place. I find it impossible not to try and predict my own future. Surely only those who are surviving from one day to the next fail to sketch out a brighter future. When I married, I truly believed that I would be alongside Sara for the rest of my life. My vows meant everything. I truly did promise to look after her whether ill or not, rich or poor. It was natural, therefore, to daydream about how things would be in the future. Where we might live; how many children we may have; our pets; a weekend getaway where we'd squirrel ourselves away from the rest of the world.

If you have an imagination like I do, then you soon find that you have built a perfect future for you both. It will all fit just as you imagine it, as long as you both share that same vision. And this was where the problems began. I chose not to share my vision of the future. Yes, we'd talk about where we would be in ten, twenty years hence. We'd daydream of future holidays together. Discuss baby names. To Sara, those conversations were nothing more than they appeared: fanciful chats over a glass of wine. To me, though, they were altogether different. To me, they were actual events that would happen. They were plans whittled in wax, soon to be set in stone. I remember them all. I remember my visualisation of the future. It was clear and transparent and well planned. It was a joint path that Sara and I would walk down hand in hand. Our goals, the same.

Wrong.

Wrong.

Wrong.

When we finally agreed to separate, the overwhelming feeling was relief. Not relief that Sara was gone; more that the plan for the future so beautifully drawn in my mind could now be destroyed for good. I had spent many years waiting for some of the things that we discussed to happen. When it became clear that our paths were splintering in separate directions, I tried to somehow fit this unexpected bump in the road into the future. I convinced myself that the bright future was still attainable. That we would still do all the things we had talked about. The plan still existed. Yes, I'd amended it over and over, but it still existed. There was always a good justification for why it just wasn't the time to try for children, or go and live overseas.

And then we parted, without incident. No screaming. No shouting. No bodies being thrown to the floor in desperation. No begging. No pleading. No crying. No kneeling *Platoon*-esque asking the sky why this had happened. Not at all. There wasn't even the merest hint of a puff of smoke, never mind an explosion. It went more like this:

"Sam, I want to talk to you."

"Yeah?"

"Come in the kitchen."

"Now?"

"Yeah."

She stood by the table, the same one on which the rings and note once lay, her arm resting against the back of a chair.

"What's up?" I said.

"You know, this," she said vaguely.

I must have given an indication that I didn't understand, because she followed up by widening her arms and saying, "This."

"Yep."

"It's not working, is it?"

"You mean the house we're in?"

"No."

"You mean being married?"

"Yes."

"Er, I suppose not, no."

I didn't really suppose, though. I knew.

"You agree?"

"Yeah, I do."

"Good. So, I'm going to move out."

"Right. Do you have somewhere to go?"

"Yes."

"So…" I paused. "When?"

"I'm going to take what I need for now. Then get the other stuff some other time."

"Right."

"That okay?"

"Sure. Whatever." (The latter word was not supposed to sound flippant and in hindsight I'm not sure that it did. It was more a 'whatever makes you happy and makes this situation less uncomfortable'.)

"Okay," she said, "I'll go up now."

It was clear that she had already mentally planned what she was going to take with her, because she was back downstairs in the hall within fifteen minutes, her case and overnight bag plump to the point that the zips were clinging on for all they had.

"Right, I'm going to get off," she said.

"Okay," I said.

Weeks passed before we even spoke again. I had nothing really to say. It seemed that the same could have been said about Sara.

When you experience some kind of serious trauma at a young age, it stays with you. It's like a ghost which follows a few feet behind every footstep – a quiet whispered sound that reminds you of your past. For the most part, it is neither haunting nor frightening. Its presence is nothing more than a reminder of unfinished business. It treads the same steps as you do to tell you that something is incomplete. That you have yet to deal with something from your past. It is also clever enough to trick you, because it makes you believe that it is the most important thing in your life. I am sure that we are all different when dealing with past trauma, but my ghost stands three times as tall as I do. An invisible, faceless apparition which gently walks behind me. It is neither friendly nor threatening. It is just there, a reminder that its presence shapes everything that I do.

Every day.

And because of its sheer size and the mystery which swirls around it like sea fog, it does become the most important thing in your life. And because this is the case, it is easy to deal with anything else life throws at you. Like no longer seeing your father or the breakdown of your marriage. They are simply cake walks.

"I'm leaving you."

Sure, no problem.

"You'll never see your father again."

That's cool. No worries.

"Your gramma is about to die."

Er, okay. What's for dinner?

After that initial trauma, nothing compares.

I can deal with everything.

I am hyper-alert.

I don't care what you throw at me.

I can deal.
I can deal.
I can deal.

Chapter 43

It is exactly ten thirty when the doorbell rings. It surprises me slightly, as I suppose I expected Sara to just walk in. We are still married after all, and this was her home for several years.

I take a deep breath, cover my face with both hands and shake my head from side to side like a dog drying off after a race through a stream. The dirty water, my memories. I stand and take the few steps down the stairs toward the front door.

I open the door and Sara stands before me. Her hair is cut much shorter, a kind of pixie-cut. She reminds me of Tinkerbell (with a lawyer's slant). I'm sure the haircut was approved by the senior partners at work and creates the right impression in front of any judge in the land. Funny how things as basic as haircuts and clothing are still deemed societally important, when clearly they are not.

She smiles, and I return it, inviting her in with a sweep of my hand.

While the kettle boils, we catch up at the kitchen table. There isn't that much really to catch up on. Our lives have become entirely disentangled, and aside from an update about a few mutual friends, there is little to say. Neither of us seems to want to delve into anything that may be controversial or outside of what we already know about each other. I have no desire to know whether she is seeing someone else or where she now lives. It just gives my imagination more to build on. It's clear from the opening moments that our connections have mostly been severed and that neither of us has any particular hunger to rewire.

I place the cups of tea on the table and she thanks me. I brought the box through yesterday and carefully emptied the contents in order on the table. The empty box sits on the floor beside me. Sara sits where Tom discovered Mum's rings and the note. I sit to her left.

"So," she says, "what have you found?"

I explain to her again what I know. I tell her that Gramma is convinced there were three witnesses. I pass her the relevant papers, one by one, and she reads through them thoroughly as if it is the first time that she has seen them, though I see a flicker of recognition each time she takes a new page. After reading each document, she places it on one of two piles in the space in front of her. I suspect one pile is irrelevant to her, the other in some way meaningful. I don't ask.

We continue in this way for an hour before she turns to me and says, "There's nothing new here, Sam."

I fear she is right.

"There always were three witnesses," she says.

I frown.

She flicks back through the pages.

"There's the woman who spoke to your mum. Silver sports car woman. That's one. There's the woman from school who had a child in the same year as Tom. She saw your mum from behind. That's two."

"Uh-huh," I agree.

"And then there's the police officer" – she finds the statement – "who saw your mum when she called in to report herself alive and well. That's three."

I nod.

"So, it's nothing new. There always were three witnesses who allegedly saw your mum after she disappeared. Two saw her at the service station. One, a police officer, saw her in person and noted it."

I shake my head. "It just doesn't –"

"What?"

"It just doesn't seem to be what my gramma was saying, Sara. It doesn't seem to fit with what she was telling me. It's like she wasn't treating the policeman as one of the witnesses. Like there was someone else."

"Why do you say that?"

"I don't really know. It's just kind of how I read the conversation."

Sara has adopted a stern look, no doubt practised at work. If she wore glasses, they would be on the tip of her nose and she would be questioning her witness by looking at them over her glasses. Eye to eye. "What exactly did she say?"

"I don't know."

"Come on, Sam. You need to do better than that. We need something firmer." There is the slightest hint of irritation in her voice, and I understand why.

"I don't know. I can't recall. Maybe it wasn't words, more...I don't know, just a feeling. Like she inferred it."

Sara sighs and pushes her chair back using the palms of her hands against the table. She pulls her hand through her hair.

"Can you ask her? Get more detail?"

"I doubt it, S. She's dying. Like, properly dying."

I swallow. The sudden emotion I feel is unexpected. Sara notices. "Are you okay, Sam?"

"Yeah, yeah." I compose myself. "I'm good."

"You sure?"

"Yep. I'm fine," I say, standing.

I sweep the papers with my hand and walk to the window. In the reflection I see the papers floating like confetti behind me. I rest my hands on the windowsill and stare at the drive, where the car wasn't *that* day.

"Sam?" Sara says again. There is a warmth in her voice.

I wipe my eyes and turn. "I'm okay, really."

She gets up from the table, walks over and stops a metre before reaching me. I turn, and she takes a further step forward and puts her arms around me. I put mine around her waist, loosely at first.

I want to explode.

I want to tell her I want to explode.

I want this to be over with.

I want the ghost behind me to disappear.

I can feel the blood rush through my veins as if there is suddenly too much of it in my body. As if my veins are overfilled, capillaries stretched to capacity. As if every part of me is inflating, my arms, my legs, my body expanding and growing. Then I feel my heart bulging and pumping, struggling to cope with the extra work it is having to do.

I feel her arms around my back and I pull her in closer, more tightly, as if she can share the burden with me, as if pushing our hearts together will somehow allow her to take on some of this pain. By the way she is holding me, I know now that she would gladly do this for me. She would share it all.

We stand silently in this position for ten minutes or more. As well as feeling that she would take the load from me, I also get the sense that there is a finality to our clinch. That we are pulling one another close for the last time. It feels like the right thing to do.

Chapter 44

Sara tells me that there are a few random bits of hers lying around the house, so I let her pick up what she wants whilst I clear the papers from the kitchen floor. I shove everything into the box and close the lid. Then I put it by the back door. I'll destroy it later.

She manages to fill two carrier bags and I don't ask what she's taken. It really doesn't matter to me. The sun drenches the hall rug and her shadow forms a shape that leads directly to the front door. It somehow seems the perfect time for her to leave.

"Sorry to say this," she says, "but you know that we need to get the ball rolling with the divorce."

I nod. "Yep, sure. I'll sign whatever you need."

"Thanks," she says.

"No problem. I reckon you're better placed to draft that type of legal stuff."

I chuckle and it instantly sounds inappropriate. I draw it back in abruptly.

"Yeah, I suppose I am," she says.

We stand facing one another for just a few seconds, and then she pulls back her sleeve.

"It's after twelve," she says.

"Right."

"Okay…"

She turns and opens the door, and we both say goodbye.

I watch the door vibrate as it closes behind her.

I wait until I hear her car leave, then I take out my phone. It tells me that I have missed two calls from the nursing home. I pull on my trainers and race down the drive, hoping that Sara has definitely gone and doesn't think I am running after her.

Chapter 45

I am out of breath when I arrive at St Dymphna's and I wipe sweat away from my forehead as I press the buzzer. A moment later I am buzzed in. I push open the door and head down the corridor, past the visitors' book and along the hallway.

I reach Gramma's room and knock lightly. There is no answer, though I suppose I wouldn't expect one. I push open the door and the room is in total darkness. There is a strange scent which I can't place. It vaguely reminds me of vegetables boiling. I am concerned about turning on the light in case Gramma is sleeping. I don't want to startle her. I stand motionless for a moment or two and then walk gingerly through the pitch blackness, my arms outstretched in front of me, feeling for obstacles in my path.

I make it to the curtains and help them back slightly, creating a small shaft of light which projects a thin, stretched diamond shape on the wall above the bed.

The bed is empty.

I pull open the curtains fully and push open the window.

Everything is as I left it yesterday.

Well, nearly.

Gramma isn't here.

I open the bathroom door and realise as I do that there is little chance of her being there. She isn't. I'm not thinking straight.

And then I am through the bedroom door and into the hallway. I head down the corridor toward the office, and as I turn the corner, I nearly knock over Jacqui, who is coming in the opposite direction. I apologise and she tells me that I needn't worry, Gramma is still with us. They have simply moved her to another room to allow for a new guest.

I see her mouth moving and I can vaguely hear her, but the words aren't making any sense. Something about a doctor. Something about medication. Something palliative. The atmosphere around me suddenly feels fuzzy, as if I am listening to her with cushions pressed against my ears. She frowns and stops talking, and then she passes me and swings open a door to my left. The third door.

I recognise Gramma immediately, though she's facing away from me, toward the window. Jacqui smiles and mouths something before leaving. She closes the door behind her.

I have seen this room so many times, but I have never entered it before. It is smaller than I thought it would be, the large window giving the impression of space that in reality doesn't exist. There is no bathroom in this room, just a small sink on the wall in the corner between the foot of the bed and the window. A small sticker on a large mirror tells me that I shouldn't drink the water. My mouth feels instantly dry.

Aside from an orange plastic chair and the bed that Gramma lies in, the room is empty. The chair doesn't look inviting and I get the impression that it wasn't chosen with extended visits in mind. It's somewhere to sit when you say goodbye. It's that simple. Don't bother getting comfortable. You won't be here long.

I notice that the walls are a dirty white, the colour of laundry that has given up trying to retain its original brightness. They are also completely empty, aside from unused picture hooks and stray nails which sit in rectangles of only slightly whiter paint. There used to be pictures, but no more. Another indication that any time spent in this room will be short.

I walk over to the window and sit on the windowsill. The sun is shining brightly into Gramma's face and I can't tell whether her eyes are tightly closed due to the sunlight or the pain you feel in your final moments. I turn and close the blind, just in case.

I pull over the chair and sit alongside the bed. I notice she is above me once again. They've moved her onto a normal bed. No fancy buttons or knobs or mechanics. It's a metal frame with a mattress. That's all. They obviously see no need to turn her, to sit her up, to move her again.

Her face is obscured by the bars, so instead I stand. Her mouth hangs open, her bottom lip protruding as if trying to catch rain. White spittle has gathered at the corners of her mouth as if to witness the final breaths being pushed through. A gallows crowd if ever there was one. The spittle attaches and detaches again with the consistency of children's glue.

I can hear her breaths but they sound different from the night before. The lowercase 'p' has been replaced by a slightly louder lowercase 'b' sound. Each breath is a struggle. I imagine her lungs desperately trying to take what air they have and force it against gravity, through her windpipe and into her mouth. The 'buh' noise is an accompaniment to the pure effort this takes. She's not trying to make a sound; from the guttural cawing to the final 'buh' release, these are the sounds of her body operating. An old machine that is finally ceasing up. Her heart, weak and rapidly reaching the end of its useful life, pumps for what it has left. As if there might just be something within her for it to keep pumping for. As if the next breath might just contain something of enough importance for her have to live through this suffering.

When I was younger, I broke my finger snowboarding. I hit a mound of soft snow, went up in the air and landed directly on my finger. When I removed my mitten, my little finger was still attached, but instead of facing upwards, it was bent fully back on itself, the fingernail nearly touching my watch face. I had emergency surgery and they stuck some pins through it and filled me full of morphine for the night. Later that night, my friends left their evening of après-ski to visit. They stayed for the allowed visiting time of three hours. Apparently, we chatted all night and I was cracking jokes and on good form. The next day, I had no recollection that they had visited. Or that I had tried to remove my drip to "get back on the slopes".

I hope that whatever dose they have prescribed Gramma, it is doing the same thing as my hospital dosage. I hope that although her brain continues to tell her heart to beat and her lungs to open and close, she has no recollection of it. I hope that the enormous struggle that her body is making is not causing her any pain.

"Buh," she breathes.

I watch the spit gather and split.

Gather and split.

"Buh."

Gather and split.

"Buh."

Gather.

And.

S

    p

        l

           i

                t.

Her eyes remain closed, the heavy skin of her eyelids holding them firmly shut. It would be too much for her brain to ask her to see. It is shutting down all but the absolutely essential bodily functions. She can no longer see. Or speak. Or move of her own volition. Her eyes have sunk deep into her skull, her eyelids lay flat. The corners of her eyes no longer run. Instead, hard grains of sand sit in small mounds, the tear ducts finally blocked.

"Buh."

Gather and split.

"Buh."

Gather and split.

I follow the lines, the endless highways of memories etched deeply into her face, each one representing a journey of joy or pain. I can see the shape of her cheekbones clearly now, triangles of bone pushing their way to the surface, almost piercing the thin skin that contains them.

I watch the artery in her neck as it struggles with its own routine. After a while, I can count the exact time it takes for the artery to pulse and then the 'buh' sound to be released. Her nightdress hangs so much more loosely than just a few days before. It is so noticeable that I want to make sure that there hasn't been some kind of mix-up. That the laundry hasn't been sorted incorrectly, leaving her wearing another resident's nightwear. A much larger woman. But I know that this isn't the truth; I recognise the lace strap which rests over her naked clavicle. Her upper ribs lie like an abandoned glockenspiel, her yellowish skin melting over each one like cheese over a burger. I pull the front of her nightdress up higher to cover what is left of her dignity. As I do, she moves.

Beneath the sheet, her legs begin to kick, and I am surprised by the force and energy that she still has within her. Her breathing suddenly becomes deeper and the accompanying sound is almost a cry now, a howl. Her toes claw at the inside of the sheet and I am not sure whether she is overheating. Once again, I freeze. Unsure what to do.

I make my way around the end of the bed, caught between pulling the sheet from her and racing into the corridor to raise the alarm. She makes the decision for me. As quickly as the kicking began, it now ceases. The cotton lies creased once again. Her breathing relaxes. She resumes the 'buh' sound.

Again and again, I stroke her forehead with my thumb, pushing back hair which does not want to be tamed. I begin to speak. It is time to let her hear what I presume will be her final sounds. Of course, I have no idea whether or not she can hear them, and if she can, whether she will understand them. But it is time. It would be far more poetic, maybe beautiful, if she could hear moonlit waves gently lapping or the sound of spring birdsong, but alas, that wasn't what was written for her. Instead, she gets me.

I tell her the things I am thankful for. The things that she brought to me. Her humour. Her caring. Her stubborn view of right and wrong. I tell her the things I am sorry for. How things were left between us. Her leaving. I tell her that I am sorry that her life has been such a struggle. That I wish I had come back sooner to see her. That maybe, just maybe, things could have been different. That maybe we would have finally unlocked the puzzle between us.

But now I'm trapped in this room, and though I am pleased that Gramma will escape the suffering, I suddenly realise that her death will do nothing to make the remainder of my life any easier.

I am still left.

I am no further along.

It feels like the dirty walls and unclean ceiling are closing in around me. I'm trapped in my memories of what happened. I am careful not to say the *actual* words, *not* to mention my father, or my mother, because the actions of at least one of my parents has defined the majority of Gramma's later life, and the entirety of mine. I don't want her to leave knowing that even to the very last breath she was still hearing about something beyond her control. I am desperate to ask her to tell me more. But she can't respond, and it feels like the pain of speaking and getting no response will be unbearable. Heavier than the weight that has held us both down for decades. It's not a step I'm willing to take.

I push down the same curl of hair for the hundredth time and watch as it jumps up again like an excited puppy. Her time is close. I kiss her forehead lightly and sink back into my chair.

I check my phone. Tom will be arriving soon.

And then I am back on my feet and I am stroking her hair again, unable to live with the thought that she may think I've deserted her. Again, perhaps? I tell her that one day I hope the story will unravel for me. That I hope that I won't always be stuck with the not-knowing, as she was. And as the words leave my mouth, I realise that we are two sides of a coin. We are not the same at all.

She won't die not knowing.

She knew all along.

Chapter 46

Back then, it seemed that a lot of things happened over what was a very short period of time. In reality, each and every day probably felt like it dragged, especially with the knowledge that closing your eyes at night was never going to bring any relief. Even when sleep captured me, it only ever took me to places which were for all intents and purposes the same as my day-to-day life. Perhaps in my dreams the scenes were more graphic. More violent. More bloodthirsty. But they were all variations on the same theme. Mum wasn't there. Dad was. Something sinister had happened. Someone had done something. Someone knew.

From the moment my father was taken away for the last time, my mind no longer allowed me to think clearly and isolate the truth from lies, the dreams from reality. I feel like my recollections of that final year have been manufactured wholly from a box of 'evidence' and an avalanche of news reports. It is very difficult to look back on your past and try to identify exactly what happened. Not only does the memory itself fade, but it also mutates to allow you to continue with your life with as clear a conscience as possible. You manufacture a past to fit with your present.

It was Red-Face and Tall who finally made the arrest on the front doorstep of our home. I would like to tell you that the incident involved helicopters and teams of armed officers who covered every possible option that a fugitive may take. I would like to tell you of barked instructions that crackled and snapped through an old megaphone. Or spotlights which threw Bond-like circles across the front of the house. But it wasn't like that.

It was around six a.m. when Red-Face and Tall told my father they were arresting him for the murder of my mother. By the time Tom and I woke, he had already been in the cells for five hours. Gramma took us into the lounge and told us that the police had made a huge mistake and had taken my father in for more questioning. She told us that they had charged him with Mum's murder, but it would all get straightened out in due course. We hadn't to worry. We had her and she would take care of us for as long as was necessary. She expected he would be home before we knew it. I don't mind saying that I think it was when she used the word 'worry' that my eyes first filled up. Tom must have noticed that something had snapped within me, because Gramma spent most of the rest of that day cradling him. He instantly regressed from a teenager into a toddler before my eyes. I have never seen that amount of emotion before or since.

Of course, Dad didn't come home.

No, Dad stayed exactly where he was. Stuck behind what I imagined were thick vertical bars of metal like in the films I had seen. I daydreamed of smuggling a hacksaw blade to him. But then, life at home was somehow less fraught. It was quieter, and the atmospheric edge that lay in every room that my father inhabited quickly began to dissipate. The rooms seemed to grow in size. There was a change in hue from grey to lemon. Gramma cleaned frantically and it made a difference. Home began to feel just that.

Outside the house, of course, things were different. There were those people in the village who would tut or sigh or frown as we passed them. Others were more vocal, more aggressive, and although my recollection is vague, it doesn't take much imagination for you to get an idea of these interactions. It has always confused me why people who have not got the slightest clue of what somebody is experiencing still believe that it is their right to state their opinion on the subject. I've given this a lot of thought. I believe it comes down to guilt. Those people are burdened with their own guilt about who they are and the decisions that they've made. They know that they haven't always acted in the best interests of those around them. They know that when they were sleeping with their best friend's husband or taking money from the till at work, they were acting in their own interests and their own interests alone. And that is not how we are taught to be, that is not how we would wish to be treated, and therefore they are saddled with an underlying subconscious guilt each and every day.

When an easy target of two teenagers and their grandmother passes by, they can make their point, they can tell us what bad people we are. Surely we must have known something? They can tell me just how bad a person my father is. And we can be branded murderers by association. These outbursts serve to make those carrying guilt feel so much better about themselves. Yes, they may be adulterers, they may be thieves, but they are not murderers, and thus from their twisted viewpoint they have clambered a few rungs up the slippery ladder of moral hierarchy.

Tom suffered the worst during this time. He was the only one who had to leave the house each day and mix with hundreds of other children at the local school. He had committed to doing so for Gramma's sake. I don't need to tell you how cruel kids can be, especially if their point of view is fuelled entirely by guilt-ridden, morally defunct parents. After only a few weeks, Tom's attendance at school went through the floor. The number of fights he got involved in went in the opposite direction. Toward the time that the case reached court, I don't think there were many people who knew where or how Tom spent his days.

For me, Red-Face and Tall were only a heartbeat behind. The friends that I'd retained began to slip away, not because they necessarily believed in my father's guilt, but rather because of the threat of the police appearing from nowhere. It was too much of a risk. None of them wanted a criminal record from something as low-level as smoking weed.

Of course, Red-Face was more than happy for me to smoke joints in the many nooks that were hidden in the sprawling woods behind the house. I have a vivid recollection of him sharing one with me one evening, somewhere deep in the forest near where Beggar's Path finally ends. In hindsight it was obvious his actions were driven by his own agenda. Though at the time, to someone of my age, he strategically positioned himself as the only person in my world that understood. He levelled with me. He knew just how difficult it must be for me. He told me about the future when this was all over. How things would get better, that this wasn't going to affect my whole life. The way he told it – so I could understand better – my future was my favourite meal. A beautiful, steaming plate of the finest, most succulent steak, pink in the middle. The crispiest of chips, dripping in oil. Grilled tomatoes and mushrooms, oozing flavour. And whilst he offered me this irresistible feast, he seasoned it with questions about the type of person my father was.

Did he ever get angry?

Could he be cruel?

Was he ever violent?

Did he and Mum get on?

Did?

Could?

Was?

Did?

Was?

Could?

The questions were beautiful in their implementation. They were dropped in at just the right time, so whilst with one breath Red-Face comforted me and told me of my wonderful future, with the next he was garnishing that same future with the outcome that he and his colleagues felt was right.

My dad must pay for what he had done.

Tall seemed to be otherwise engaged. He only appeared from time to time. And each time he was there to apply pressure. To tell me how serious the situation was, that they needed me to tell them more about my father. What about my grandparents, he asked. What was my grandfather like? Was I afraid of him? How did he treat my father? Tall seemed to like the answers I gave to these questions. After all, I was only being honest. And they told me enough times that if I wasn't honest, then they would find it difficult to turn a blind eye to my days spent smoking in the woods.

Gramma, Tom and I quickly realised that the

only safe place was inside our home. The world outside our walls was empty of friends and full of hate.

Eventually, as that year passed, I began to see Red-Face and Tall much less. I had already been into the police station several times, going over and over (and over) the things we had talked about. They took down my statement, typed it up and sent me away with a copy. They seemed happy. Then they wanted to go over it again. It wasn't quite right. They needed a few changes. It was like handing in schoolwork for marking and checking and it being passed back to me with *suggested* amendments. After three or four goes, they were very satisfied with my final submission.

It wasn't until a few weeks before the court case that they began to arrive again. This time, it was Tall's turn. He seemed keen that I remember exactly what my statement said. I read it over and over. He banged his fist on the kitchen table when I got parts wrong. He told me that in court I would be asked many questions and it was vital that I remembered what I had told him. It was important that justice was served. All I was doing was telling the truth about my father's character and personality. It would be up to the jury to hear all of this evidence and decide for themselves. I was simply helping them to understand what day-to-day life was like. They wanted the truth, that's all, he said.

The paradox was that Tall wanted my memories of the truth, while Red-Face gave me the weed that helped me to forget everything each time I smoked it.

Chapter 47

Outside the court on the day that my father was convicted, our family had already been sucked in whole and spat out in pieces. It was the equivalent of a family being fed through a wood-chipper.

My mother was long gone.

My father was now gone.

Tall and Red-Face stood alongside Tom and me, guarding us from the journalists who thrust phones into our faces, jabbing them forward like angry geese, asking us to comment. We stayed quiet, as we were told to. Tall stood on the steps, and when the crowd quietened he told the world that they were pleased with the outcome and that justice had been served. He asked for (what was left of) the family to be left alone and given privacy.

We didn't know it at the time, but somewhere further down the pavement, my gramma was providing a comment for a similar-sized group. I would find out later, on the early evening news, that she believed that there had been a "tremendous miscarriage of justice" and that her son "simply wasn't capable of murder". She also insisted that she would not give up fighting. Not till her final breath.

We never saw Red-Face or Tall again. They had what they wanted.

The next few weeks were even more of a haze than the previous year. I don't remember much of what happened. My time was spent in my own room and Tom's. We didn't go any further than the garden. It wasn't worth it. People still shook their head and tsk-ed as they passed the end of the drive. Journalists still appeared for comment. They wanted to know how it felt to have a family split between guilt and innocence. How it was that we could still live with Gramma when she had the opposing view to us. After all, they said, I was an integral part of getting my father convicted. Tom and I stopped leaving the house. We smoked until we passed out in the conservatory. We drank the crates of beer that Dad had piled up in the garage. At first, we hid it from Gramma and then...well, one day it no longer seemed to matter.

And it was clear to her that there was nothing she could say or do to deter her two teenage grandsons from doing whatever they wanted. I clearly remember that the fresh lemon-coloured rooms in the house quickly began to revert to their unhappy greyness. The atmosphere once again blackened. A suffocation, like smoke billowing from a factory. It even became difficult to breathe. Gramma became a ghost in her own home. The meals she prepared were pushed away. Her words were ignored. She began to fade, to disappear right in front of our eyes. It would have been the most poignant of magic shows if anyone had bothered to notice. Her control over the household fell from ubiquitous to nothing in less than a few weeks. The house itself seemed to agonise over its inhabitants and before long it made no attempt to be a home. Just a shell for living in.

And then, perhaps when it became a reality that Dad wasn't suddenly going to walk through the door, that he wasn't going to tell us all that it was a big mistake, our lives hit a new low.

I remember that day well, because you don't forget days like that. Regardless of your state of mind. Days like that stay forever inscribed on a part of your brain that does not forget. The memory is stored as a reminder of how bad times can get. And what caused the bad times. In this case, I have always believed, it was Gramma.

I have to say that I don't know what the exact day was. That doesn't mean that my recollection is tainted; it just didn't seem like the actual day of the week mattered, especially when every day followed a similar pattern. I do know that it must have been a few weeks after my father's conviction, because the knocks on the door had become scarcer and the smartly dressed presenters and their small camera crews had all but left the end of our drive. We were old news and, unless something changed, our story was over. You pretty soon realise that once the journalists have had their fill, they quickly leave to set up temporary home at the end of someone else's drive. After all, there is always another town, another husband, another murder, another weapon around the corner.

If I am to tell my story correctly and you are to understand it, then I must tell you every single detail I can remember about that day.

Chapter 48

It was a 'normal' day in our new your-father-is-a-murderer post-conviction life. I got up around ten thirty that morning, feeling unsteady from the night before. As usual, I spent a few moments in the bathroom splashing cold water on my face in an attempt to tell my body it was time to engage in another purposeless day. My eyes were bloodshot, but I put that down to lack of sleep. It was easy to tell myself that it was nothing to do with the previous evening. In all honesty, I don't know whether it was or not. By that time, I didn't usually remember much of the day before, especially those last few hours of the evening. The hours between passing out on the conservatory floor and somehow making my way up the stairs to bed.

I dragged myself down the stairs, my balance telling me to feed the bannister through both hands like I was pulling a small boat to shore. My head snapped and fizzed as small incendiaries popped and exploded in the endless corners of my mind.

It hurt.

As I neared the bottom step, I could hear that Gramma was already in the kitchen. I paused for a moment. I think if I hadn't, the dizziness and nausea would have overtaken me and I would have fallen face first onto the hall rug. I listened as her spoon near-silently cut through the milk and scooped up what I imagined was cereal. I heard her slurp and quietly crunch the contents of the spoon, and clink the spoon against the perimeter of the bowl. I listened as she repeated this three or four times.

Then everything went silent. I don't know to this day whether she had finished the cereal or whether she had an inkling that I was standing only a few feet away, but her chair abruptly screeched backward along the kitchen floor and she got to her feet. A combination of naivety and my inability to think straight meant that I was still standing in the same pose at the bottom of the stairs when she appeared at the kitchen door.

"Morning, Samuel," she said. She wore the type of nervous smile that people wear when they have no idea what reception they may get.

I grunted.

"Did you sleep well?"

I shrugged.

"Breakfast?"

I stared at her. I knew that Gramma was trying to be the woman she'd always been, and that made me angry and resentful. Why in the world was she trying to be the woman she'd always been when the world was no longer the same place? Surely if everything changed around you, then you too had no choice but to change? In fact, by not changing, weren't you by definition changing anyway? Tom and I had discussed this to varying levels of success every day and every night as we smoked. I was in my late teens – legally an adult – by now. And of course, I knew everything. I would state my cosmically energised theories about Gramma and Dad and Mum to Tom all day, every day. He was a captive audience and was almost duty-bound to agree with me. A sergeant and his lieutenant. Master and servant. Unwittingly, I brainwashed him.

"Samuel?" she said.

I continued to stare.

"I asked if you wanted any breakfast?" It was little more than a speck of irritation that crept into her voice. Indistinguishable to the human eye. But not the human ear.

I know I pulled a face; disgust was what I aimed for.

"Why are you –"

"Why am I what? Why am I what, Gramma?" I spat.

"Why are you being like this, Samuel?"

"Like what?" I shouted. "Like –"

It was her turn to cut in. "Like a spoiled brat. Like a spoiled little boy."

"Spoiled? Ha, I'm fucking spoiled? My mum's dead and my dad's a murderer. Yeah, right. I'd like to see what my life would have been like if I hadn't been so spoiled."

"Shut up," she snapped.

I had never heard her speak like this before. Ever. For so many years I'd wanted her to say the same words to my father or Gramps, but she never did. She never stood up to them. She cowered away like the coward she was. Let them say and do whatever they wanted to her and to Mum and to Tom. How dare she think she could suddenly begin to speak this way to me?

"What?" I felt my fist curl.

"I said shut up," she repeated more firmly. I think, in hindsight, the tone of her voice shocked me more than the actual words. Before I could speak, she continued.

"Shut. Up. And listen to me. Right now."

I did.

"Why don't you grow up and set an example for your brother? And you can start by stopping smoking that rubbish."

"Grow up?" I shouted.

Tom appeared from the lounge. He looked nervous and stood with his shoulder resting against the door frame. I could tell from his eyes he'd been up longer than I had. They were red and bloodshot and his eyelids hung heavy.

And that was it, I was across the hall in less than a second. A few feet away from her.

"Sam!" Tom said.

I ignored him. "Grow up, Gramma? I need to grow up? My dad is a murderer – he killed my mum. I've lost my mum and my dad. Don't you get it?"

She arched her back and lifted her shoulders. It gave her a little extra height. I'd seen it on wildlife documentaries. She stood her ground. It was nothing more than masquerade and mimicry.

"Yes, I get it. But I've lost my son and my daughter-in-law, and I'm not about to lose my grandchildren too."

"*Your* son," I spat, "is a fucking murderer. He ruined my life. And Tom's."

Tom looked at the floor.

"He might be many things, Samuel. But he isn't a murderer. Can't you see? The police, the courts – they're wrong."

I saw tears in her eyes. I was gaining control.

"So," I said, pushing out my chest, "you're telling me that all these people are wrong. Your precious son didn't do it."

"Yes," she said, suddenly assertive again.

"So where is my FUCKING MUM?" I screamed.

And then it all happened very quickly. I remember moving in more closely, my wiry frame towering over her. Her forehead inches from my mouth. I could instantly feel her fear and I regret to say, I enjoyed it. I know I had my hands raised, but that was only to make myself look more threatening. Nothing else. I'm sure it was. I saw her suede-lined moccasins shuffle an inch or two backwards.

I felt Tom pull on my arm, which took me by surprise, and heard him shout no, or something similar. I spun, and then spun back. And then Gramma was on the kitchen floor. I saw her fall – more of a crumple than a fall. She seemed to fold back on herself concertina-style and then she was on her back. I saw her eyes. Wide and open.

And then I got down to her level and Tom pulled back on my arm, which ended with a clenched fist. I tried to shake him free, but he had both his arms gripped around mine and because he was still standing he had the height advantage. We struggled for a few moments as he repeated my name over and over and over.

"Sam, no. Sam. Sam. Sam. Stop...Sam. No. Stop. Sam, stop...Sam. Sam. Stop...Stop...Sam, Sam."

And then, as I loosened my arm from his and pushed him backwards, he shouted:

"Sam, no, you're not Dad."

And I stopped. I pulled myself backward, clambering to my knees and then falling back, finally coming to rest in a sitting position. My arms dropped to my sides without my instructing them to do so. My large frame, which moments earlier had cast a shadow over Gramma, was reduced to something a tenth of the size. I folded like an umbrella.

And then I covered my eyes with both hands and began to cry.

And behind me, sprawled out on the rug near the hat stand, Tom did the same.

I could hear Gramma's sniffling and whimpering a few feet ahead of me. Echoing off the kitchen tiles.

Chapter 49

Gramma moved out of the house the following day. Her sister came to collect her. We didn't say goodbye. In fact, we didn't say anything. She stood in the hall and waited for the three pips from her sister's car, then she picked up her suitcases and gently closed the door behind her.

Tom and I lasted a few more years together, until, at the first opportunity, he left too. London was indeed calling.

Chapter 50

"Buh."

The spit gathers and splits.

"Buh."

Gather.

Split.

"Buh."

I squeeze her hand again. Her eyes remain closed. The only sign that she is still with us is the repetitive sound that she forces out. It is clear that there isn't much time left now. I check my phone with my left hand, which brings on instant guilt. It's just before half past two.

There are various notifications, but I ignore them. They will have to wait. This sets my mind whirring as I imagine what the messages and calls could be. It takes all my concentration and focus to switch my mind back into the room where Gramma lies.

There is a light knock at the door, more of a warning that somebody is entering than a request to enter. The door immediately squeaks open. Jacqui enters the room, explaining that she just needs to perform a few checks and issue further medication. There is a brief stand-off until I realise that she expects me to leave the room.

Reluctantly, I let go of Gramma's hand and whisper that I won't be long. I want her to know that I'll be here right to the end. It is the least I can do. As I kiss her forehead again, I am sure I hear her murmur. For the briefest of moments I am filled with hope that she will speak.

"Buh."

I smile at Jacqui. She returns the smile, and as I leave the room I hear the tear of Velcro and hope that the circumference of Gramma's arm is still wide enough for her blood pressure to be taken.

I am only in the corridor for a matter of seconds before Susan comes out of the office to greet me. I am surprised by her appearance, which seems too perfectly timed for a lifelong cynic like me. I check whether there is one of those angled mirrors people have outside their driveways near the office door to give a view of the corridor. There isn't.

"Your money," she says, holding out folded notes to me.

"Thanks," I say. I take them from her and feel the slightest tension until they are finally released into my hand.

I unfold the notes and count them in my hand. Nine notes. One hundred and eighty pounds.

"That okay?" Susan asks quickly, obviously noticing the confused crease which runs vertically between my eyes.

"Er…"

"What?" she asks with similar speed.

"Er, I'm just confused. I think there was more. And receipts."

"Receipts?"

"Yeah, I keep all my receipts in my wallet too. There were loads."

"Well, what do you need those for?" she snaps.

"I don't. I just wondered –"

"Here," she interrupts, nodding toward the double doors I've yet to go through.

We walk into the small corridor and wait for the double doors to come to a stop. It smells strongly of ham and pea soup, and I realise that the kitchen must be down here, along with the emergency medical room. It seems a strange combination. For a moment, I wonder whether ham and humans have the same smell when reduced to broth form. The bubble of thought is popped by Susan, who encourages me into a corner.

"Listen," she says, "it's all there is. All I could find. There were no receipts or anything else. Just the cash."

"But it was all together, in the wallet."

"This had fallen out on the bottom of the safe."

"What, just the cash?"

"Yes," she snaps, "just the cash."

"So, the receipts?"

"I don't know."

I can't believe that I am having this conversation in the last few moments of Gramma's life, and again my paranoia kicks in, taking me to a place where Susan planned this, knowing that I'd want to cut the conversation short. It seems less than appropriate to be arguing over money, or till receipts for that matter.

"So, this is it?" I say.

Susan has turned red, from what I presume is a cross between anger and embarrassment.

"That's all there was. On the floor of the safe. Near the back."

"Okay." I don't have time for this. "Well, thanks."

I try to move away, but she stops me with her plump red hand.

"It's not the first time we've had this happen," she says quietly. "It's Tony. Things keep disappearing. He told me about the missing money and I said I'd investigate. A day later, this just appeared in the safe."

"Okay," I say again, trying for a second time to move toward the double doors. She grips my arm.

"Tony is the nephew of the owner," she says, her eyes scanning the ceiling. "You see? He's the nephew. I can't say anything. I'll lose my job."

"Right."

"Please don't say anything, Mr Darte."

I pull away from her and push open the left-hand door. I'm halfway through the door when I feel her hand on my shoulder. I turn.

"Here," she says, and pushes another twenty-pound note into my hand. I think people call it a sweetener.

I take it and let the door swing behind me.

Chapter 51

I stand outside Gramma's door for a few moments, trying to tell by listening whether Jacqui is still on the other side.

I hear nothing and push the door open.

I am as surprised to see Tom as he is to see me. He instantly rises from the plastic chair and smiles. We meet awkwardly at the end of Gramma's bed and embrace in the small amount of space we have. He smells of cigarettes.

We part again, each taking an awkward step backwards, to take a better look at one another. He looks like shit. It is clear his long hair hasn't seen a brush for at least forty-eight hours. His eyes are dark and heavy, his skin red and puffy. He is wearing a baseball shirt, white with a giant red-and-blue 'C' covering one breast. What is left of his black skinny jeans looks painted on, except where his knees have broken free of the fabric. The Converse baseball boots look like they were from the very first production run. Early twentieth century. I am sure the soles are only held on by the moisture trapped in his chewing-gum-white socks which peep warily over the top like curious meercats.

We find ourselves on either side of Gramma's bed, which feels even stranger, so I walk around to his side. He sits back in the chair and I sit on the floor against the wall, facing him.

"Good to see you, Tom," I say. And it is.

"You too, man," he says. The smell of alcohol drifts to floor level. "She's not good, man."

"I know," I say, and for the first time I notice that the 'buh' sound has ceased. I get to my feet.

Gramma is lying on her back, facing the ceiling. I can vaguely make out the lightest of breaths being pushed from her mouth. It is near soundless, and more like a rattle than an actual breath. The sound comes from something vibrating in the back of her throat. There is nothing left of her now. It is simply a breath being pushed up through an empty vessel. She has been reduced to a jumble of bones held together by nothing but a shroud of useless skin. And through the middle of this mass, a solitary breath is sucked in and then out.

Tom stands alongside me, his hand on my shoulder blade.

Gramma sucks in another breath. And we wait to see whether it will be blown back out again.

I begin to stroke her forehead.

"It's okay," I whisper, "it's okay. It's okay. It's okay, Gramma."

She breathes out.

"It's okay. It's okay, Gramma. You're not alone. I'm here. Sam. Samuel, your grandson. I'm here. You're not alone."

And in.

"You're okay. And Tom's here too. Thomas. Your other grandson, Thomas. He's here; he's come from London to see you today." I realise I am speaking to her like I would a baby, but it seems the natural thing to do to keep it simple. I continue: "Haven't you, Tom? Haven't you come to see Gramma?"

I have to look at him.

She breathes in.

"Oh, er, yes. I'm here too, Gramma," he says quietly. "I'm here."

He looks back at me, and I nod toward Gramma.

He takes her right hand in his. I am sure I see her fingers curl slightly.

"I'm here, Gramma. It's Tom. Thomas. I'm here to visit."

I'm surprised to hear his voice crack, and he removes his hand to wipe his eyes on his heavily tattooed forearm. He takes her hand again.

"I'm here. We're with you, Gramma," he says, "me and Sam. We're here."

And out.

There is a crackle as she sucks in another breath, like the sound of dry sticks on a fire. I see her eyelids flicker, the skin so thin that I am sure I can see the rise of her irises. I can certainly see her eyeballs moving behind them. Her tongue crawls along her bottom lip, toward the corner. It rests on a pile of white sticky spit. Then she pushes out all the air that remains inside her.

"Buh," she says.

I continue to stroke her forehead until long after it is clear that she can no longer feel it. There doesn't seem to be a good time to stop and I am grateful when Tom finally lifts my hand away.

We turn to one another and embrace again.

This time I pull his chest as close to mine as I can. I want our hearts to touch. I want to take any pain or suffering that he feels inside into my heart instead. He grips my back and rests his head against mine.

I think we are both surprised by the tears that meet between our faces and gather and run down my neck.

My phone rings in my pocket.

We both listen until it stops.

Chapter 52

There is a lot of activity in a nursing home when a resident dies. It's not something I've experienced before. The designated nurse (Jacqui, in our case) confirms that Gramma has indeed died. She pulls up the sheet so it rests just across her shoulders. Then she tells us that we can stay with Gramma as long as we want. She leaves, and Tom and I stand in silence for what seems like the longest time.

Eventually, a doctor arrives and also confirms that she is indeed dead. I don't think it took much medical training on his part to come to this conclusion. He too tells us that we are welcome to stay as long as we want.

About ten minutes pass, then Tom breaks the silence.

"How long do we stay for, Sam?" he asks nervously, looking for guidance. He sounds just as he did on the morning he found Mum's note.

"I dunno," I say.

I've never done this before and I quickly scour my memory for something I may have watched once that might give me an indication. Is there a length of time you stay in a room with a deceased relative? I remember people throwing themselves onto corpses, begging them not to leave, but I don't feel that way. I also have a vague recollection of families all congregating around the deceased. Like a final goodbye. The problem is that Tom and I are the only family she had. Certainly the only available family. And we're already here.

Another ten minutes pass, and I turn to Tom.

"Shall we go?" I ask.

He nods, his eyes telling me he's thankful that I am calling time on this.

I lean over and kiss Gramma for a final time.

It just seems like the right thing to do.

Chapter 53

We return home from St Dymphna's late afternoon. It feels good to have Tom back. The house seems to instantly come alive with his presence.

Tom begins by wandering around the house – 're-familiarising himself' is how he puts it. I follow him upstairs first, where he spends a few moments in each room. I watch him take in all four corners as if for the first time, looking behind the door, treading across the carpet to stand idly at the window and take in the surrounding area. I wonder whether it is the years of substances that have made such familiar surroundings so unfamiliar. It is either that or he has successfully blanked out this life he left behind.

I follow him into his old bedroom, which is pretty much how he left it. Clothes still on the floor, Built to Spill and Silver Jews posters up on the wall, his collection of rocks on the windowsill. The collection he told me would be worth a fortune one day. There is even his Zippo on the floor by his bed. He reaches down and picks it up. He snaps the lid and it bursts into flame.

"Awesome," he says, apparently pleased with the lighter. "What the fuck, Sam? It's like I never left."

I smile. It hadn't occurred to me at any time to change anything in the room. It was easier to just close the door. The door that still has the car registration plate sign: 'T0MS R00M'.

"Ha," he says, snapping the lighter again, "it's like I'm one of those people who go missing. Like their parents leave everything just how it..."

It feels like his words disappear in front of my eyes, and silence engulfs the room.

"Fuck," he says, noticing the macabre irony of what he was saying.

I felt it at the same time as he did. We both look at one another. I'm not sure whose face cracks first. I don't suppose it matters.

Our laughter does.

It starts as a tiny blown raspberry, and as the light shower of spit is still travelling, we begin giggling and then laughing. The more that we look at one another, the more we laugh. At one point, Tom has to cover his eyes as he turns away in a dramatic spin. For a moment he looks every bit the rock star. When he turns back, I am still laughing and he starts again. And eventually, he creases and his legs suddenly no longer want to stand. Then he sinks to the floor, still laughing and holding his stomach, his shoulders twitching.

"What the fuck? What the actual fuck?" he eventually manages to get out. There is no time for me to answer. "What the actual fuck?" he laughs again.

I don't need him to explain. I know exactly what he means. What the fuck? What the fuck is all this (raises hands to the heavens) about? What are our lives about? Whose fucking idea was it to bring us into this incredible joke of a life? I mean, seriously, who has this fucking life?

And all of this comes through in his laughter. It is hard to describe exactly how that laugh feels, but it isn't far from incredulity. Whoever programmed the lives of Samuel Raymond and Thomas Raymond Darte had no idea what they were doing. This whole existence is a sick joke. Who decided that it was sensible to butter our lives with so much trauma? So many unanswered questions. Such an impossible ending.

For both Samuel Raymond.

And Thomas Raymond.

It takes us about half an hour to recover from the breakout of laughter and make our way back downstairs. Tom follows me into the kitchen.

"Drink?"

"Beer?"

"Sure."

I had expected this. I pull out two bottles of Hop House 13 and flick the lids. I pass one to Tom.

We both drink at the same time.

"Cheers," Tom says, looking at the table.

"Cheers."

"Same table, eh?" he says, his finger idly running straight lines across the area where he found the note. And the rings.

"Yeah. Same table. There's only me here."

I shrug.

He shrugs too.

"Yeah, man. I meant to say sorry about the Sara thing. Sorry about that."

"It's okay," I say. "You've said it a hundred times."

"Ah, okay," he says.

He looks relieved, and I'm glad. It was nice to hear him mention Sara. And though strictly it *was* the first time he had mentioned her, it felt nicer to let him think otherwise.

"Weird to be in here," he says.

"I'm used to it," I say. "It is what it is. I suppose."

"What happened, Sam?"

"When?"

"All of it. What in the name of…well, fuck knows, happened?"

He pulls a tin out of nowhere and opens it, placing the lid on the table. He begins to build his cigarette. He nods at me to ask if I mind, and I nod back with a look of 'no problem' on my face.

He then pulls some foil from inside his coat pocket and unwraps it on the table. "Northern lights," he answers, without looking up.

He breaks up the weed and lays it on top of the tobacco. Then, with conjurer's hands, he rolls, licks and lights the joint. His lighter snaps shut. Then he takes a long draw and holds it for as long as his lungs allow, before exhaling it into the low light of the kitchen, forming a blueish-grey mist that leads from his mouth to the ceiling.

"In simple terms," I say, taking the joint from him, "Dad killed Mum. Got sent to prison for it. Gramma supported him. We didn't. Gramma died."

He nods. "That's about right."

Chapter 54

I find out over the course of that night in the kitchen that Tom *is* actually in a band. He's the lead singer and guitarist. A pretty good one, it seems. They're called Inertia and have got a US support tour set up. Nothing too big, but all the major cities. Twenty-six dates. It also seems that he *has* met the people he tells me he has. He shows me his phone contacts with names that even I recognise. He shows me pictures of himself standing, or in some shots jamming, with some famous faces.

He tells me about his girlfriend, Nina, and that he has been faithful to her for four years. He's worried about leaving her behind, and it seems that she shares the same worry. She sounds like a very nice person. The more he tells me about her, the more I like her.

We play music from our past. We smoke. We sing.

We sit opposite one another at the kitchen table and I notice that we both have a need to make physical contact. Each time one of us leaves for the toilet or to grab another beer, we seem to make sure that we touch as we pass one another.

A hand on the shoulder.

A pat on the back.

None of it seems real. Sometimes touching makes it easier to believe that it's tangible. And, to me at least, if it's tangible, it's real.

We drink beer. We laugh. God, do we laugh.

He tells me of the times he's fallen offstage too drunk to stand; that the drugs are "a bit" of a problem, but he minimises it so much that I instantly decide I needn't worry; that he tries not to think about his life before London. It's sad to hear, but I understand.

Completely.

Another beer. Another smoke.

The evening is going really well until Tom's elbow slips, which releases his chin to the edge of the table. There is a cracking sound, and for a moment I worry that he's actually broken some part of his jaw. It turns out the sound made it seem worse than it was. He rubs his jaw and chin numerous times, switching between hanging his head between his knees and stretching his neck far out backward. It is on one of these journeys up that he notices the box in the corner.

"What's that?" he asks, peering through reddened eyes.

"What?" I say, hoping my question will be enough of a deflection for him to lose his thread.

"That, there," he says, swinging his head gently toward the corner of the room. Then he sits up straight as if he is standing to attention and says, "That box, there."

I quickly realise that I am absolutely out of my depth. This guy has drunk beer with the drummer from Mötley Crüe. He isn't going to lose his thread that easily. It is clear that the intake of the evening isn't having anywhere near as much of an effect on him as it is on me.

"I dunno," I say unconvincingly.

"You do," he says, slightly teasing.

"I don't," I say, raising my eyebrows.

He stands up. "Come on, what are you hiding from me?"

I stand too. "Nothing," I say, placing my hands on his chest. "It's nothing, honestly, just a box of old papers."

This seems to calm him. I feel his muscles relax under my hands. I have an overwhelming urge to protect him. He is all I have left.

"What papers?" he says.

"Just…just old papers, Tom."

"About what?"

"Nothing."

There is a distinct moment when all sound seems to stop. Then it instantly restarts.

"Ah," he says, smiling. "It's the old court shit, isn't it? Stuff about Dad. Mum. Yeah?"

I feel him tense again, so I let him pass and I sit back down at the table.

He goes over to the box and takes off the lid. He pulls out a fistful of papers and partially fans them out in front of him. I watch his eyes studying the papers, jumping from one to another, focused and set. Like an owl pursuing a mouse. As I watch, the Longpigs sing 'On and On'. It feels like a soundtrack for this moment. I wonder why they never made it bigger.

Tom throws the papers back into the box and tosses the lid on top. He stares at the box for a fraction of a second, then walks over to the table and drops onto his seat.

"You been through all that again, man?"

I nod, watching him carefully.

"Again?"

"Yeah," I say.

"I told you," he says, leaning in, "it's not worth it. It's a form of torture."

"I know."

"Shouldn't put yourself through it, man," he says, shaking his head. "It's not right."

"I know," I say.

I explain that it was driven by Gramma's health and my concern that we'd lose all her knowledge and past recollections before she died. She may have just had the final clue, and maybe, just maybe, she held the answer to the puzzle we are trapped in. As it happens, she didn't. He nods and I think he understands.

"We'll never know," I say.

He nods again.

Chapter 55

It's only as I turn off the kitchen light that I pick up my phone. It has been sitting in the darkness on the shelf next to the speaker.

There are five missed calls.

All from the same number.

The same person.

I switch the screen to black and put the phone in my pocket. I'm glad that I didn't see what I've just seen earlier in the evening. Or, worse still, imagine if Tom had seen my father's name appear, all brightly lit, on the table in front of him. We would have had an entirely different evening.

No, I don't think Tom would have reacted well to that.

Not at all.

Chapter 56

34.48
-0.12

I'm awake before the sun and I'm at my desk. It takes less than the twelve minutes that MySnug records for me to send an email to my supervisor letting her know of my grandmother's passing and that I won't be working that week. I log off again.

My feet are cold, and it seems far too much effort to drag myself back to bed. I push back my desk chair, stand and then flop onto the sofa like a child post-tantrum. I push my feet into the corner of the sofa, where it is actually colder than the current temperature of my feet. But I rub them together and generate some heat, before toppling a number of cushions to form a canopy above them.

I take out my phone and scroll up and down the screen idly. The calls from my father began at three thirty-seven the previous afternoon, the last at nine thirty-one.

I scroll through messages and calls, doing a

general spring clean. I quickly bore of my phone, and turn to face the sofa cushions in a vain attempt to make it darker. Darkness is a companion of sleep, and I pull a cushion from under my head and place it over the side of my face, covering my eyes. Then I close my eyes and repeatedly make wishes that sleep will swoop down and take me for a short while. If not, it'll be a very, very long day.

I adjust my sleeping position more than a hundred times until I realise that my mind isn't interested in sleep. I turn over and face the desk. The clock tells me that I have been attempting to sleep for nearly two hours. It's seven thirty. I turn back over and return the cushion to my head. It is then that I hear shuffling coming from the hall. I remember that Tom is still here.

"What the hell?" he says lazily.

I know at that moment that all hope of sleep has ended and my day has begun.

Tom has always been that way. A kind-of 'I'm up, therefore everyone is up' attitude. I speak through the cushion.

"Morning, Tom."

"What the hell are you doing, man? Looks weird."

"What?"

"You lying there. No head, no feet. Like a fish prepared for dinner."

I laugh as he pulls the cushion off my face, then feign that the brightness is blinding.

"Get up," he says, "come on."

He pulls the cushions from my feet and tosses them onto my body. All of a sudden I feel ready for sleep. I push my face deeper into the sofa.

"Nah, I'm tired," I say weakly. I know this will irritate him.

"Come on, Sam. Get up."

I'm silent.

"Sam. Come on, man, get up," he says, his patience thinning. "I'm a guest. Get up."

"A guest?" I laugh. "Seriously, Tom?"

He hits me repeatedly with the cushions, over my head, my face, my body. "Will you get the fuck up?" he laughs.

I turn over and face him, smiling. "Okay, okay, okay..."

"Come on, 'cos I need coffee," he says, and I watch as he disappears into the hall, I assume on his way to the kitchen. I push my face into the sofa and close my eyes.

"And don't even think about going back to sleep," I hear him say over his shoulder. I hear his lighter snap as he passes through the hall.

Chapter 57

We drink coffee as the sunlight makes its way along the kitchen surfaces and cupboards. I get the feeling it is looking for something.

The coffee is an attempt to shift the feeling of emptiness that alcohol always leaves. I get the feeling that Tom suffers less than I do with the morning after. He is lively, animated, open. It is a pleasure to see. He reminds me of Mum.

We talk about the past; we talk about the present; we know better than to talk too much of the future. We are both acutely aware that there are too many factors that can affect *that*.

Tom tells me more of his struggles and I tell him of mine. I wonder if he is feeling the same way that I do. I wonder if he is filled with regret, yet hope. I wonder why I haven't been there for him through all of his problems. I am grateful I have the chance to change that now.

My phone vibrates near-silently in my pocket. It's happened three times over the last few hours. I am concerned that if I take it from my pocket, I will affect the flow of our conversation. This happens all of the time now. In fact, it has become socially acceptable. I've lost count of the number of conversations I've had that have been reduced to ashes by the interruption of a phone call or message. It is the summit of ignorance and rudeness. I have often thought that if someone kept interrupting a conversation in person, you'd ask them to leave or be quiet or worse. But because the interruption comes through a little handheld computer, the entire human race has accepted it. And so quickly. Virtual interruptions weren't even possible twenty years ago. Oh, how the human race evolves!

We could be locked in some deep conversation, maybe about to open up about some desperate fear or seemingly insurmountable problem, and instead a screen is thrust in front of us and we have to smile politely at a picture of a surprised-looking cat near a cucumber. It is unbelievable. The number of truly worthwhile moments that have been spoiled by the interruption of mobile phones is limitless.

I am fortunate that as my phone rings once again Tom has just left for the bathroom. He blames his constant visits on the coffee. I take the phone from my pocket. As expected, it's my father. I am in two minds whether to take the call, but something drives me to answer. At the same time, I get to my feet and push the kitchen door almost shut. Then I make my way to the furthest corner of the kitchen and speak.

"Hi?" I say, prepared for an enfilade of abuse.

There is a slight crackle on the line.

"Hi?" I repeat.

"Oh, er, hello." The voice sounds uncomfortable, maybe distracted. "Hello. Er, is that, er, Samuel? Samuel Darte?"

"Yes it is," I say, glancing at the door.

"Hello, er, Mr Darte. Can I, er, call you Samuel?"

"Sam's fine."

"Thanks. Hi, Sam. I have, er, a call for you from Paul Madden, the, er, governor here. Can you take it, please?"

"Sure."

The line crackles again and then I am greeted by the far more assertive tones of "Mr Paul Madden, Governor, HMP Basham". He confirms my name again and asks whether I am the son of Raymond Anthony Darte. I confirm that I am. He lists the prisoner number as well, but it means nothing to me, so I just agree in the hope he will get on with what he has to say before Tom returns. He tells me that he is sorry to have to telephone with the news that he has. That my father, prisoner number whatever, was found dead in his cell the previous afternoon. He cannot confirm for sure at this stage, but he is pretty certain that my father's death was from natural causes. There was no sign of any foul play, but "all that will be cleared up with the postmortem". He tells me that he is sorry and that the prison will be in contact after the postmortem. I'll also be able to collect my father's belongings in due course.

Tom pushes open the kitchen door just as Mr Madden asks me if there is anything further he can do. I tell him no and thank him.

"Everything okay?" Tom says, smiling.

I nod.

I have no idea what the answer to his question really is.

Chapter 58

I'm glad to have the evening to myself.

Tom fancied a few beers for old times' sake and called up a couple of friends in the city whom he'd kept in touch with. He's not sure what time he's coming home. I tell him that the spare key is still under the same pot at the front of the house and again decline his offer to join him. Tonight is for me.

I open the fridge and find a beer right at the back behind a large tub of natural yoghurt that saw its best day a few months before. I take the bottle and wipe the ice from the label. For a moment, I'm Howard Carter, discovering something precious and a little unexpected. I hope I don't meet the same fate. I flip the top and take a drink.

The box is where it was left last night, and I pick it up and push open what has always been known as the kitchen corner door with my shoulder. On the other side is a small porch which leads into the back garden. I place the box on top of a wooden chest and search through the mess of old coats until I find the hook that holds the single key for the back door.

I recognise my father's old rain jacket and fleece, my gramma's Sunday coat. I haven't been out here for a long time.

I unlock the back door and take the box through the door and up the steps to the top corner of the garden, where the hole remains. I nip back inside and collect my beer and the lighter that Tom left behind. It is a warm evening and the birds are out, chirping happily above me. It's way past their bedtime. I'd like to think that their shrill cries are their way of trying to share the truth with me, but I am not sentimental that way. Life has taught me not to be. The birds are out looking for food and twigs and scraps for nesting. Nothing else. My presence is nothing more than a threat to them.

I throw the box into the hole and sit back on the pile of dried mud and soil. It crumbles between my fingers. I have been to the hole a number of times over the years (at one stage I almost filled it, but lost interest after a spade full or two). This is the first time, though, that I've really sat and studied it. I am struck by how well my father dug it originally. The sides have eroded over the years, and of course the police dig probably expanded it significantly, but it is still possible to see the compacted soil where my father would have dug. The more recently turned soil at the bottom of the hole that the police picked and sieved through is loose, its colour noticeably different to the rest. This is where the box sits, crumpled and torn, its contents spilling from the sides. I take another swig of my beer and jump into the hole. I'm surprised how deep it is, and for the shortest time I wonder how I'm going to get back out.

I tear the box apart and separate some of the pages, screwing them up, spreading them around my feet. I snap open Tom's lighter and begin to randomly light pages around me. Within seconds flames lick the side of the box, and I notice the bulk of the papers that remain in the box begin to surrender to the exigent heat. I kick my foot into the side of the hole and clamber to the top.

I collect dried branches and sticks from the garden around me and throw them on top the papers, to stop them escaping. Then I sit back where I was before. I sip my beer and watch as the flames hungrily devour the contents of the box; watch as the contents go from white to red to brown to black. As the smoke comes from the hole, a light wind diverts it away from me, in the direction of the woodland. It seems that even nature is on my side today.

Chapter 59

The fire is still smouldering as I open my curtains the following morning. Sad-looking smoke swirls gently from the hole. The blaze is over, and the smoke hangs in the air like a straggler at a party who doesn't want to leave but knows that the main event is finished.

I stretch and let out a loud sigh to accompany it. I can't remember a time that I slept so well. It is already bright outside and the clock tells me it's a little after ten. I pull on my pyjama bottoms and an old football shirt and yawn. Something seems different today. I'm not sure what it is, but it feels like relief. Am I allowed to feel this way? Is it okay to feel relief when two of your closest next of kin have just died?

I don't know.

Maybe.

I don't think there are any specific rules on this. And anyway, if there are, they probably don't apply to my life. Few people are qualified to say how you should act when your mother is murdered by your father, you meet your estranged grandmother after two decades and then both your father and grandmother die within twenty-four hours of each other. I'd challenge anyone to tell me exactly how I should feel right now.

My overwhelming feeling is relief.

And that's what I'm going to run with for now.

I'm also not sure who is judging me.

Aside from myself.

I leave my bedroom and pass Tom's closed door. It could be some time until he emerges. I was asleep when he got back the previous night, so I have no idea of the time he finally crashed in bed. I am surprised that he didn't drag me out of bed to share a joint or two with him. I'd expected my door to edge open and to be greeted by his crooked smile partially lit by the moonlight. He'd already have a smoke in his mouth, unlit of course, and he'd coax and persuade me to get up and spend time with him "for old times' sake, man". I'd refuse at first, playing along with his game, knowing all the while I'd be up in a matter of seconds to be in his company.

The house also seems to feel my relief. The walls seem a little wider, a little taller, as if they are pushing out a deep breath. The secrets and lies and bitterness and sadness they have held in for all these years can finally be released. I make my way downstairs, stopping at the window where the stairs turn back on themselves. Grey smoke drifts gently by before becoming transparent in the freshness of the sky.

I walk into the kitchen and I am greeted by a parallelogram of warmth provided by the morning sun.

"Hey, man. Coffee?" Tom asks.

I jump slightly. I didn't expect to see him.

He is sitting at the kitchen table. In front of him lies an ashtray, cigarettes, his lighter and his phone. His mug is empty.

"Yeah, sure," I say.

He walks over and puts the kettle on. He squeezes me around the waist as he passes. It doesn't feel awkward. When the cafetière is full to the brim, we take it over to the table and sit in the same seats as the day he arrived. The day that Gramma died. The day that my father died.

"Good night?" I ask, plunging the coffee.

He scoops three spoonfuls of sugar into the bottom of his cup in anticipation.

"Yeah, y'know, it was pretty cool."

I get the feeling it wasn't.

I pour the coffee, and he stirs in the sugar. No milk.

"Yeah?"

"Well..." he says.

He tells me that nothing stays the same. In fact, he theorises, it is an impossibility for it to do so. The only way that things would stay the same would be if nobody ever moved on from the moment in time they were presently stuck in. It would take the entire world to stop for this to happen. And then, well, who would want to be constantly stuck in time? He tells me that life is about creating moments for ourselves and sharing them with as many people as possible. We should always do exactly what *we* want, as long as it causes no pain or suffering to others.

I am staggered by his monologue and wonder whether he has practised and used it before. It sounds so polished, yet it sounds like the words he is using are coming to him spontaneously. I watch as he speaks and, just like the house, he seems new and clean and fresh and somehow expanded. His presence seems all-enveloping. The years that I have thought of him as an addict, a liar, a waste of space feel as distant as Jupiter. Sure, he has problems, but I'd advise you to check the veracity of anyone who tells you they haven't.

He tells me that the friends he met the previous evening are, of course, not the same. They have changed. The connection has broken. These people are intrinsically linked to his past; they represent a snapshot in time. They are just a Polaroid. There is no doubt that the past is important; after all, these friends got Tom through a time when he needed somebody. And yes, he admits, their lasting legacy is his addiction to weed and cigarettes and alcohol and whatever else anyone is offering. But, in the years after my mother went missing, he needed people who were happy to escape into a haze of smoke every day. And for their own reasons, those people became his friends. And now, the circumstances have changed. Some are married, others have children, and like Tom, they have changed too.

"It's a fact of life," Tom says. "Can't change it. You move on."

I nod, again taken aback by his words. His outlook.

He leans forward and takes a cigarette, and I hear the snap of his lighter.

"The worst thing anyone can do," he says, and fills his lungs with an enormous amount of smoke, "is to look backwards. We can retain memories as long as we don't live in them, y'know. We shouldn't yearn for a past that's already gone and can't be changed."

He breathes out and I watch the blue smoke collide with a million dust particles.

It almost looks artistic.

"To yearn for a past that's already gone," he repeats thoughtfully. "I like that. It'd make a good lyric."

He picks up his phone and taps it in to remind himself.

Chapter 60

We spend the majority of the day in the kitchen catching up and discussing our lives. And what remains of them.

Late afternoon, the desire to drink comes on suddenly for Tom. A flash of panic crosses his face when he realises we don't have any alcohol. He literally cuts off our conversation mid-sentence and stands and announces that he wants a beer. It becomes an immediate and vital quest to get some.

I let him walk into the village alone, and twenty minutes later he is back, his face relaxed, his finger as good as on a ring pull as he walks through the front door. He smiles and tells me he drank one on the walk back. I return the smile; he has already taught me in the last forty-eight hours not to make a judgement.

Tom passes me a beer and shoves the cans into the fridge, still inside the carrier bag. He suggests that we sit in the remaining warmth of the day, so we take our beers with us to the hole at the top of the garden. I show him the remains of the box and he smiles knowingly. Then he jumps into the hole and snaps his lighter. Moments later, the unburnt pages are ablaze.

He climbs back out and sits alongside me on the pile of dry mud.

"Been a long time..." he says.

I'm not sure what he is referring to, but I nod.

"...since I've been up here, man. Remember when Dad dug it?"

"Yeah," I say.

"What the fuck?" he says.

I agree. It is something that is lost forever now and can't be brought back. I accept that we will never, ever know why he dug the hole in the first place.

Was it for Mum? Probably.

Will we ever know? No.

"D'you know, a part of me thinks that he did it just to wind the police up," I say, licking amber bubbles from my top lip.

A wry smile crosses Tom's face. He nods slowly. "I never thought about that," he says.

"Wouldn't put it past him," I say. "It's the sort of thing he'd do. He thinks he knows better than everyone else. That he's smarter..."

Tom turns to me. "Y'know, you could be right."

"Maybe."

At that moment, the fire crackles and a flurry of burnt paper circles us like a murder of crows. It's something I may have taken as a sign a few days earlier.

"Didn't fucking work for him, did it?" Tom says.

We both laugh.

I'm a breath away from telling Tom the news from the prison, but I decide against it. This isn't the time. I don't know when the time will be, but the last thing I want now we've reconnected is for Tom to find out that I have been secretly communicating with Dad over all these years. I need time to consider exactly how I will share the news. It doesn't seem sensible to blurt out something that I haven't completely thought through. Especially after a couple of beers have loosened my tongue. My overwhelming desire is to protect Tom. He's been through enough.

"You still good at drawing?" he says, switching the subject.

"It's been years," I say.

"Must be like riding a bike, y'know."

"Why, what's up?"

"I need a logo for the band. Ours is just lettering. I think we need a logo. Like the Stones' tongue and lips. That kinda thing. Something iconic. Thought you could do something."

"Okay." I'm interested. "Maybe like something in a circle? Y'know, like the old anarchy 'A' or the sixties' peace sign?" In my head, a circle kind of seems to fit.

"Nah, not a circle, man. I hate circles."

"What?"

"I hate circles, Sam. Anything but circles."

"The Who had a circle. So did Guns n' Roses." I rack my brain. "Strokes? Public Enemy?"

He shrugs. "I still hate circles. They're ugly. They don't fit neatly alongside each other. There's always a space between them. Always a gap for things to slip through."

"Foo Fighters?"

"Exactly," he says. "Says it all, Sam. No circles. It's a trap. Like a hamster in a cage. Never movin' on. Just repeating its mistake. Over and over."

"So never moving fits with Inertia?"

"No circles, Sam." He looks at me seriously. "I don't trust them. Round and round and round. With no end."

"No circles then?" I say, smiling.

"No circles."

Tom pats me on the thigh and tells me he won't be a minute.

He isn't.

He returns with four more cans and passes me one. I finish the one in my hand and throw the empty into the hole with the rest. The flames momentarily seem interested in the metal, before getting back to the sticks and papers.

Tom passes me a joint and I hear the rush of bubbles escape his fresh can. I open mine and draw deeply from the joint. My chest feels instantly lighter. As if gravity no longer applies. Tom holds up his can and nods to an invisible presence somewhere far above.

"To Gramma," he says.

"Gramma," I repeat, pointing my can in the same direction.

"Never thought I'd say that," Tom says.

"Nah, me either." I take another draw and pass him the joint. "She didn't have it easy, did she?"

"She supported *him*, though."

I tell him what I know. About Gramps. About their marriage. That it wasn't that easy for her. That she lost her entire family by supporting Dad. That she was full of regret – not that she had supported him, but rather that the broken relationship between us was not repaired earlier. That she was resolute to the end that Dad hadn't killed Mum. It was her opinion. She couldn't help it if that was what she believed. If anything, she should be applauded for never wavering. Even if it destroyed our already fragmented family.

"Can you remember that day when you hit her?" Tom says.

I am shocked by the comment and I swallow my mouthful of beer quickly to avoid spitting it out. I burp and wipe my mouth on the back of my arm.

"What?" I say.

"When you hit her. Y'know, in the hall?"

I am stunned. This isn't my recollection.

"She fell," I say incredulously. "I didn't hit her."

"Okay," he says, lighting another joint.

"What do you mean, 'okay'?"

"Nothing, man."

It's quiet for a moment and we both stare into the ashes of our past.

"D'you think I hit her?"

"Nah. Forget it."

"You do, don't you?"

"Well," he says, "it was a long time ago, but that's what it looked like."

He tells me his memory of the afternoon: of me squaring up to Gramma; of me pushing her, and then pulling back my fist and hitting her. Hard. In the jaw.

"I thought you'd killed her for a minute," he says.

I have no recollection of this.

"And then," he continues, "I had to pull you off. I thought you were just going to keep hitting her until... y'know."

"I would never have hit her," I say.

"You did. I absolutely remember you doing it, Sam."

We both stare into the hole again. The fire laps and curls at what is left of the papers. I feel my past disappearing. I take another drink.

"I'm sorry," I say. I have no reason to dispute his version of events. Sometimes we build our own version of the past. The accidental trip and fall seemed to fit me best.

"What for?"

"Everything."

His brow creases.

"Everything. Everything you've been through.

Seeing that with Gramma. Just...everything. I should have protected you better."

"Nah," he says, "you don't need to apologise. You were young, y'know, not as clued up. You did all you knew to do, and we didn't have the fucking luxury of parents to guide us. Don't beat yourself up, Sam. It's done. It's the past."

I am grateful for his words.

I can't help but think that as his older brother it should be me saying these words to him. Finding the correct words to help him through. But that all seems unnecessary now. It's clear that despite his dependencies, he is much further down the road than I am.

Unlike me, he has dealt with our past.

And now he is dealing with his present.

At least we both agree that the future isn't worth thinking about.

I pull him close, holding his neck in my open palm. He does the same and our foreheads touch.

He feels like my brother again.

Chapter 61

I wake early the next morning and instantly curse myself for drinking.

I have a headache, specifically in my temples. It feels like someone is forcing large drawing pins into my skull at either side. Strangely, it feels a little better if I apply pressure to each side.

Anxiety fills my chest in the form of a thousand tiny pistons which pump up and down at alarming speed. This is the worst part. The tachycardia. I feel pity for my heart – a strange paradox, given that it was me who put it in this position.

This is why I rarely drink.

I lie for a moment, considering the day ahead. Then I throw back the quilt and climb out of bed. There is no point in taking myself down the equivalent of a bottomless well. I have a headache. I feel anxious. That's where I am, and I know that when I see Tom he will tell me to get on with it. That it's not forever. Deal with the present, man.

I dress and make my way downstairs.

Unsurprisingly, Tom's bedroom door is again closed.

I am surprised to find the kitchen so tidy. Everything washed and cleared away. The work surfaces wiped down. The draining board sparkling. There, on the table, trapped under an ashtray, is a note. I've been here before.

I take the note from the table. The handwriting is messy and scrawled, like the author was gripping the pen in the same way a toddler would hold a crayon.

Hey Sam
Had to get back to real lIfe. Loved seeing YOU man. WIll be In touch. TAKE It EASY.

I smile and place the note back on the table. It seems like an apt way to end what I believed was going to be a chapter with no end. It's the world's longest chapter closed, and in fact I now realise that my story only really has three chapters.

Life with Mum.

Life after Mum.

Life after Dad.

It's that simple. I am just hoping that the third chapter will bring less of the unknown and unsolved. Less suffering and more focus on the things that really matter. The important parts of life.

The final chapter is what I make it.

I get the feeling that it will be far happier than the first two.

Chapter 62

A couple of days later, I return to St Dymphna's for what I expect will be the last time. I have to collect whatever possessions Gramma has left, and deal with some paperwork regarding care home fees and a death certificate.

The sun has been shining almost constantly since Tom left. Bright, almost piercing sunlight has kick-started spring into life much earlier than usual. I stop myself reading anything into this. It is what it is.

As I take the short walk to the home, I stop to admire the gardens of the rows upon rows of semi-detached houses. Almost everywhere I see tiny shoots of life. The bulbs that have been lying dormant for just under a year are pushing their pointed spears toward the blueness above. I know it must be my state of mind, but they really do seem to be stretching. Raising their green arms in approval. Each and every leaf is a celebration. They seem to be saying: "Sam, you made it, you got through. Nice work."

It feels like a gift from Tom.

Though Tom himself seems like a gift.

I constantly remind myself not to dwell on the past. It is difficult after all these years, but I am committed to changing my mindset. Altering my well-worn neural pathways. The events of the past cannot be changed. Only the present matters. And I control that.

I've yet to tell Tom about Dad's death. It's on my list; I just want to find the right time. I want him to get back to his girlfriend and his band and his friends first.

Settle back in.

Focus on his tour.

Have some time to contemplate our last few days.

I no longer want to be the person who only rings with bad news. With sadness. With frustration. I want my name to appear on his phone and for him to smile.

Something tells me that this will happen in the future.

And then I pull myself back in.

The present is all that matters.

Forget the future.

The door is ajar when I reach St Dymphna's and I let myself in. The corridor is empty, so I sign in and make my way towards Gramma's room. As I pass, I notice that the door to room three is closed. I wind my way down the corridor and reach her room. I am just about to let myself in when Susan appears through the double doors. She looks flustered.

"No, no, no," she says breathlessly. Her cheeks look warm enough to fry eggs.

"Sorry?" I say.

"No. You can't go in there," she says. She's finally caught her breath.

"I've just come to collect my gramma's belongings. You left a message for me?"

"Yes, yes, I know. Follow me," she says.

I do.

She takes me back down the corridor, past the third door and through the fourth door to the end of another corridor. Finally, we go through a glass door into the dining room. It's the type of glass that is made with thin strands of metal horizontally and vertically forming hundreds of small squares. It's security glass, and I wonder for a second how many residents have tried to break in or more likely, out of the dining room.

The room is long and wide. There are maybe a dozen rectangular tables, each covered with a plastic checked tablecloth and surrounded on the long edge by wooden chairs. Bottles of ketchup, glass salt and pepper shakers and a small pile of napkins sit centrally on each table. It reminds me of a seaside fish and chip café. At the far end is a large bay window shaded by a huge sycamore tree stretching in the street outside.

"Sorry," Susan says, "we're understaffed. And one of the residents on the upper floor…"

She pauses for a brief moment and then chooses to end her sentence by running her finger across her neck, sticking out her tongue slightly and closing her eyes. It seems entirely out of place.

"Oh," I say. "Er, sorry."

I'm not sure what I'm apologising for, but I suspect it's probably on behalf of Susan.

"Anyway," she says, turning flippantly, "here you are. Take what you want."

There is a box on the table behind her. It's neither large nor small. Just in the middle. The type of box you'd maybe get a new printer in. The box is brown and plain, so I can't tell what it originally held. She watches me carefully as I pull open the flaps to get inside.

I turn to her, my frown telling her that something is wrong.

"Sorry," she says, "but I have to stay with you while you go through Mrs Darte's belongings. It's company policy."

I ignore her and turn back to the box.

"Where are all her clothes?" I say without looking at her.

"Oh, they went on day one. Didn't think you'd want old women's clothes, so we got them off to charity."

"Right," I say quietly. I'm not sure I would have wanted them, but it would have been good to make the choice.

I rummage through the box, which pretty much contains four or five cuddly toys, a few pictures and some books.

"Her jewellery?"

"She's still wearing that. She wanted to be buried in it."

"How do you know that?" I say, again refusing to turn around.

"It's all in her notes. She told us when she first came here. We have to follow our residents' wishes."

I don't like her tone.

"Okay."

I turn, holding a grey toy rabbit whose ears flop when I shake it in front of her slightly. "So this is basically it?"

"I'm afraid so," she says.

I turn back to the box and take out the pictures.

My father and mother on their wedding day.

Gramps looking distinctly unfriendly, standing outside a bed and breakfast in some English coastal town. A sign hangs behind him. No Vacancies.

Me and Tom. We are holding hands and smiling in the back garden. Tom looks about four, which would make me eight or nine. In the background, you can just make out my parents, sitting on uncomfortable-looking metal-framed deckchairs. They too are holding hands.

"Okay," I say.

I leave the home with a grey rabbit under my arm and the picture of Tom and me in my hand.

It seems like a strange combination to be leaving with. I'm not sure what I expected, but if anybody asked me what remained of my gramma, I don't think I would have guessed this.

Chapter 63

As I reach the edge of the small car park, I hear my name, my full name, being called in a quiet whisper from behind me. I stop and turn, and see Tony following me. He holds up his hand to ask me to wait. He reaches me a moment later.

"Mr Samuel Darte," he repeats as he gets close. He is wearing his new jacket again.

"Hi," I say.

"I just want to say sorry to you. Sorry about Mrs Joan."

I see his eyes fill instantly as he says my gramma's name.

"Thank you, Tony," I say. I have a sudden urge to fill the distance between us and hug him, or at the very least shake his hand. I do neither.

"Mrs Joan, she is gone, and I am sad for this. Sad for you."

It is clear that to Tony my gramma wasn't just another name, just part of his job. She was a living human being whom he saw almost daily over a period of six years. She was someone whom he got close to and shared time with. She mattered to him. I am grateful for this. Up until the last week, Gramma probably believed that Tony was the only one who cared, and perhaps she was right. I suspect her answer would be different if I could ask her the question today.

"Thank you," I say again.

"Mrs Joan, she talked about you. Many times. She would be happy you came."

There is enough in this sentence to tell me that my decision to go to the home was worthwhile. I would have brought some lightness to her weight. No matter her beliefs, she got to spend time with her grandson in her final week. For a second, I realise that Tony may hold information regarding my mum. Perhaps Gramma told him something that was relevant. I push the thought away, hearing Tom's words: *Forget the past.* I know he is right.

"That's good," I say. "Thank you, Tony, for caring for her."

"It's no problem to me," he says, wiping his eyes with the ball of his palm.

"Okay, well, you take care," I say, and edge slowly toward the street. He lets me take a few backward steps and then immediately catches me up.

"One more thing, if okay," he says quietly.

"Uh-huh?"

He glances toward the door to the nursing home and then back to me.

"Your money," he says.

I nod gently to encourage him to continue.

"Your money. From the coat. Susan give you it back, right?"

"Well —"

He wasn't looking for an answer.

"But Susan take some of the money. She keep it."

"Okay..."

"She takes all of your money and throws tickets away."

I assume he means receipts.

"When you say money is missing, she has to go to put some back, but she doesn't have tickets anymore. They are in bin. Gone. So she puts some of money back and give to you."

"Are you sure?" I have every reason to believe Tony's version of events.

"I'm sure. She do it many times. Over and over. I see her."

He turns to the door again. The coast remains clear.

"You cannot tell. I lose my job."

"But you're related to the owner," I say. "You can tell them about what Susan is doing."

He looks puzzled and then his face clears. "No, no, you get that wrong. Susan husband owns the home. He is the big boss."

"Ah, right," I say.

"Please," he says, holding his palms together in front of his face, "I need job. For my wife. For my baby. You won't tell big boss that I tell you?"

I put my hand on his upper arm and squeeze slightly. "I won't," I say, "I promise."

"Okay," he says quietly, nodding his head. "Okay. Okay. Thank you, Mr Samuel. I'm sorry."

"It's okay." I smile. "It's not your fault."

He returns my smile and continues to gently nod his head. I tell him I have to go. As I make my way through the gate and onto the main road, I still feel that he is watching me.

Considering whether he did the right thing by telling me.

Wondering whether I am trustworthy.

Worried for the family he needs to feed.

I don't turn around, but if these are the thoughts that are orbiting within his brain, then he can rest easy.

Whatever I decide to do, I won't bring Tony into it.

Chapter 64

I let myself into the house and place the photograph and rabbit on the sideboard in the hall. I enter the kitchen, but then think better and go back into the hall and sit the rabbit up, his back against the table lamp, his ears hanging on each side of his head, his eyes no longer obscured. I place the photograph centrally, so in the evening the light from the lamp will spotlight Tom and me.

I spend the afternoon making the type of calls you have to make when somebody dies. With the death of my father, the number of calls I need to make has doubled.

I speak to the prison, who tell me that my father did indeed die from natural causes. One moment he was there, the next gone. It's that simple. They ask me what I want to do with his body. I tell them that they can do want they want with him. Nobody will be attending a funeral.

They thank me and tell me somebody will be in touch. It is still my responsibility, as next of kin, to pay for whatever the prison needs to do. I tell them that I understand and I am happy to pay for whatever it is they do. I ask them to keep it as cheap as possible. It's what he deserved.

I call Tom to let him know that Gramma's funeral will take place Thursday coming. I already know before I tell him that he won't be attending. He has too much to do before the tour begins and can't be away from the band again so soon. I understand and I'm relieved. It saves the pressure of trying to arrange some kind of send-off that neither of us wants to be part of. It would feel disingenuous to suddenly make a fuss over someone whom neither of us knew for the majority of our lives. The funeral will be a simple occasion. No words. They would only fill the room with their emptiness.

It feels like the right time to tell Tom about Dad. There is a long pause, then he breaks the silence.

"Fuck. Okay," he says.

"You okay?"

"Yeah, sure. Just seems weird, y'know. Dad and Gramma dying, like, basically at the same time."

"I know. You and I are the last ones standing."

"The only ones left," he says.

"The survivors."

He laughs quietly. "Yeah."

I tell him what I've agreed with the prison and he agrees with me. Let Dad go out with what he deserves.

Nothing.

Chapter 65

There are only three of us in the room.

And one is dead.

The registrar spends the few moments that I stand alongside Gramma's coffin desperately searching the high walls and deep-pile carpet for something to look at other than me. All the seats are empty. No one has come.

The only word I speak is "okay" as I nod to the registrar.

She pushes a circular button on the wall, and the curtains close around Gramma's existence.

She is officially gone.

Another footprint washed away by the rain.

Chapter 66

The morning after the funeral, I am woken by the sound of Mum's voice. Her song has never sounded so crisp, so clear. So pretty.

It is coming from downstairs.

It is the sound of pure crystal glass.

Of precious stones.

Of innocence.

I can't work out her song from my room, so I get dressed and make my way slowly down the stairs. I stop halfway to hear her voice. She is singing an old Squeeze song that she used to sing to me when I was younger. A story about a man and a woman and a baby. In the end, the woman and the baby escape the man.

I can suddenly relate.

Her voice seems to get closer, then further away. As if she is cleaning and dancing and skipping all at the same time, the hall rug as her stage. I so want to turn the corner and watch the finale, but I know better. I have been tricked too many times before. I know that her song stops and she vanishes as soon as I look. So, I stay where I am.

As she reaches the final climatic part of the song, she sings out the familiar riff as if she is a guitar or keyboard.

And then, all is quiet.

And the only sound that can be heard is one man clapping.

I am asleep on the sofa when I am awoken by a loud knock on the front door. At first, I can't be sure whether it was real or part of the dream I was having, so I lie and stare at the ceiling. Waiting.

And there it is again. A loud thumping as if whatever is outside absolutely cannot wait. The knock has a frantic sound about it. As though whatever it is, it is about to expire. Like invisible ink. Or a message that self-destructs.

I drag myself up from sofa and make my way to the door.

"I thought you'd be in," the woman says.

I'm not sure why. I don't ask.

"Are you okay?" she asks. She must notice my vacant look because she continues, "It's Anne. From the park."

I'm still not sure.

"With the dog. Digby. He came and sat on you, on the bench, remember?"

It makes sense. The woman from the woods whom I spoke to briefly. The one who from a distance sounded like a witch. She smiles when she sees my look of recognition. She looks different without the hat and the big coat and the dried mud and the dog. Though I expect most people would.

"Yes, I remember. Sorry, I've just woken up."

"It's okay. Don't worry. I've brought you these." She thrusts a small box of chocolates into my hand. "I wasn't sure whether flowers would be appropriate." She giggles nervously.

I take them from her, not knowing why. Before I can thank her, she continues.

"I'm sorry to hear about your nan. I just wanted to let you know that if there's anything I can do..."

"That's very kind," I say, "but I think –"

"I'm so sorry about how things worked out, Samuel," she says.

I smile.

"I'll tell you right now, though, that if you ever need me to tell my story again or to stand up in court or whatever, then I'd be happy to do it. I know what I saw that day."

I hear Tom's voice. I know what he would tell me. *You're already free from this. Live for now. Forget the past; you can't change it.*

"What do you mean?"

"I'm sorry," she says, "I'll start again. I'm Anne. Anne Chapman. I was one of the people who saw your mum in the days after she disappeared. I saw her in the Lakes. I was walking with Fleet, the dog I had before Digby, and she was coming the opposite way."

"Right?" I say warily.

"She was with another man. Not your dad. She tried to look away, but as we passed each other our eyes met and she gave me the tiniest of smiles."

This doesn't make sense. I don't recognise the woman. Or her name. It wasn't on any of the papers in the box. I'm sure of that. Anne Chapman. Anne Chapman. No, I'm sure of it. I've never heard the name before.

"Are you sure?" I said.

"Definite. I know the date because I was only away walking for that weekend, so it couldn't have been any other day."

"Did you tell the police?"

"Twice," she said, "and then they told me they'd call if they needed to. They never did, though. Time went by and...well, it seemed they'd solved it."

"Right," I say, "that's interesting."

I take down her number and thank her for her time. And for the chocolates. I close the door and sink to the floor, resting my back against the wall. Thoughts flood my mind, and it's only a matter of minutes before they utterly overwhelm me. Like a bucket under a neglected tap, my mind is already overflowing.

Across the rug, on the sideboard, I notice the grey rabbit's ears have fallen over its eyes.

Chapter 67

Chapter 68

Chapter 69

Chapter 70

Chapter 71

Chapter 72

Chapter 73

Chapter 74

Chapter 75

Chapter 336

I never did do anything about that knock on the door back in the spring. I considered it for a few days, and I nearly called Sara for her opinion, but I decided it was better left as it was.

Perhaps for my own sanity.

Perhaps because of the words Tom spoke.

I have only managed to see Tom a couple of times since Gramma died. He's been busy – the tour went well, and now his band are recording their first record. They're also using the logo that I drew on their merchandise. We speak at least once a week now.

Sara and I finalised the divorce back in August. We remain as good friends as is possible for any couple who has been through this type of thing. I think it is nice to tell people we are still friends; it's a way of saying that I am magnanimous and mature enough to be able to move on; that we can be in the same room without screaming. Not that we ever screamed. And not that we have been in the same room since. I've not spoken to her since we were together at the house, poring through the papers in the long-since cremated box.

I sit at my desk watching the snow begin to melt and fall from the washing line outside. In the top right-hand corner of the screen, my weekly time quota slowly ticks down on MySnug. Changing jobs is my next goal. You can't just overhaul your entire life in six months.

Some things take time.

Chapter 337

My phone vibrates on the desk in front of me.

I don't recognise the number.

I pick it up.

"Hello?"

"Hi."

The voice is quiet, shaky. And vaguely familiar.

"Hi?"

"Is that Sam?"

"Yes," I say.

I hear a long exhalation at the other end of the phone. Then, the sound of gentle weeping.

"Hello?" I repeat.

"Hello, Sam," the voice says. "It's Mum."

THE END

About The Author

M Jonathan Lee was born in Yorkshire, England where he still lives to this day with his two children. He regularly dreams of writing an album, and wakes to realise that he can't sing nor play an instrument.

His first novel, *The Radio*, was nationally shortlisted in the Novel Prize 2012. *337* is his sixth novel.

HIDEAWAY FALL

web: www.hideawayfall.com
twitter: @hideawayfall
facebook: /hideawayfall

LEE

ALSO BY THIS AUTHOR

THE RADIO

THE PAGE

A TINY FEELING OF FEAR

BROKEN BRANCHES

DRIFT STUMBLE FALL

Praise for M. Jonathan Lee

"Very cleverly done, and I guarantee you will want to re-read it again once you get to the end, and know the full story. The first 5* review I've given this year. A fantastic and brave story."
Andrew Webber, author

"Original and inspired. Excellent."
Milly Johnson, Sunday Times Bestselling author

"I listened to all of it, which these days I only do with books I don't want to put down...a very good writer and also darkly funny... all [the] characters came to life on the page."
Trisha Ashley, Sunday Times Bestselling author

"Totally absorbing. Another page turner."
Michael Fowler, author

"A Tiny Feeling of Fear" may well become your new favourite book. It certainly is mine."
Nick Jones, author

"...actually perfect."

Michael Carter, author

"The 'twist' at the end is believable but impossible to guess. Read this book."

Mark Jackson, author

"First class... an excellent book."

Kathryn Hughes, Sunday Times best-selling author

"Remarkable... an amazing story of family life."

Harry Dunn, author

"An excellent read."

Robert Weston, author

"Beautifully told delicate tale of loss, grief and guilt."

Bloomin' Brilliant Books book blog

"Lee has created perfect characters, surrounded by an intense, and at times chilling plot. Five Stars."

Whispering Stories book blog

"Beautifully written and absorbing. I highly recommend it."

Linda's Book Bag blog

"Amazing debut novel."

Secret Manda book blog

"I love books like this — there are so few books out there that I find genuinely creepy in this way, and I love it when I stumble across one."

Jo's book blog

"A fantastic book which is comparable to The Unlikely Pilgrimage of Harold Fry and Lost and Found. You should all go and buy it now!!"

Shell Reads' blog

"Then BOOM, holy smoke the ending really wasn't what I was expecting. I'm not going to say anymore on that matter but it totally blew me away."

It's All About The Books blog

"Poignant, honest [with] a perfect plotline."

Belgian Reviewer blog

"Wow - this is such a beautifully written, powerful novel which, though not action-packed, really made me feel like I was inside the head of someone feeling so trapped and unhappy. It really spoke to me, and I feel that this is such an important book to read."

Laura, snazzybooks.com blog

"The writing flows from the page in terrific style – one of those books you live while you are reading it, and will stay with you when you are done... I am quite sad it is over."

Liz Barnsley, Goodreads

This edition published | 2020

First published | 2020
1 2 3 4 5 6 7 8 9 10

Hideaway Fall publishing
BBIC S75 1JL UK
www.hideawayfall.com

ISBN | 978-0-9954923-5-6

Set in Century Schoolbook MT

Lyrics reproduced by kind permission of Tom McRae (c) and
(p) 2000 db records and 2005 (c) (p) Sony/atv Music Publishing
Limited ASCAP | Cover designed by Hot Frog
Original art by Paul Morton| 2020

Printed and bound by Charlesworth Press | 2020
Visit www.mjonathanlee.com | www.hideawayfall.com

LEE

a novel by m. jonathan lee

Light me a smoke
I'll tell you a story

I feed on fire and confusion
Of this crime I'll rid my soul
I told my troubles to the river
She shared them with the seas
She returned them to me doubled
The river holds no offer of peace

Like a snake eating snake you confuse me
Who's killer?
Who's captive?
Who's free?

– Tom McRae

Chapter 1

From a place high above the clouds, all you can make out is an expanse of green. The colour is deep, almost bottle, and from here it looks like the velvet upholstery of old dining chairs you'd find in a stately home or colonial house. It looks so soft you want to reach out and touch it. You want to push the brushed fabric in the wrong direction. Mess with its beauty.

As you pass through the wispy clouds (which persevere in trying to spoil the perfect summer's day) you can see that the ground beneath is actually covered in squares of varying colours and sizes. Blues and yellows and reds all thrown down haphazardly across the land, like playing cards in a game of pairs strewn across the floor. Each is different, yet each very much the same, and all are surrounded by an area of green before the next one begins.

As you drift closer, you can make out movement. At first you could be forgiven the triteness of using a word like 'ants' or 'insects' to describe them. But such nouns have been used to death by humans

travelling on planes or hot air balloons or standing atop skyscrapers or whatever. By the time you have a chance to consider this, and indeed another noun, it is too late. It is clear that the grey, non-descript shapes — which move slowly, like oil in water – are humans. And lots of them.

You notice that the grey shapes are grouped together. They gather around the squares, and those without squares sit instead in circles. They walk in twos, in threes, in fours. Some move quickly; others, stretched out, long and thin, don't move at all.

You are getting close now, gently floating as carefree and relaxed as snow falling from a cottonwood tree. You are able to make out the scene beneath you more clearly. You can't yet see the faces of the people below, but you can make out their shapes. Their shapes and positions. Groups of people are gathering around what it is now clear are multi-coloured blankets, to eat in the open and celebrate the beauty of this near-cloudless day – to walk, to sit, to reflect, to play games, to talk, *to be human* and take in the warmth from the strange ball of fire which exists somewhere out there in the blackness of space and keeps them all alive.

Your eyes dart in all directions, naturally following sudden bursts of movement or unusually bright squares. You focus, but just for a moment, before something else catches your eye. The pattern repeats over and over, and you wonder what it is

exactly that you are supposed to be looking for. And at the moment you wonder, it all becomes clear.

There are now less than thirty squares in your line of sight. They are laid out at different angles, some positioned as diamonds, others perfectly straight. Most are predominantly blue, red or green. Or a chequered combination of two, or all three.

One stands out from the rest.

A yellow blanket.

And that is the one you choose to focus on.

Soon, all you can see is the yellow blanket, surrounded by a moat of green, the edges of nearby blankets just encroaching on the edges of your peripheral vision.

Around the blanket you can see six people.

That's us.

Me and my family.

Just the six of us.

If you had joined us three years earlier, you would have also met my grandparents on my mother's side. But they've gone now.

So now there's just my remaining grandparents; then me, my mum, my dad and my brother.

From here, we are perfectly normal in every way. We look the same as the rest of those surrounding their squares today. We eat the same food. We breathe the same air. We share the same skies.

You couldn't tell from this snapshot that everything would be different for us. You wouldn't

have guessed that within a day of this vision of warm cordiality my mother would disappear.

Like a puff of smoke.

Gone.

Chapter 2

We gather annually for the family picnic.

I am told that in years gone by up to thirty family members would attend. That was back in the days when most of the family lived on the streets of endless terraced houses which surround the park, all within a couple of doors of one another. They would gather on the first Sunday of July each year (which was the tradition, though nobody can now remember why) and eat, play games and spend time together.

I have a vague recollection of playing badminton in the humid, windless summer days when I was much younger. I remember large, park-wide games of hide and seek with perhaps twenty participants. But the day of the picnic that I am describing to you is far more mundane. Family members have long since given up making the effort to attend. Many have died (and therefore could be forgiven for their absence), whilst others simply didn't pass on the tradition to the next generation.

On that day, there are just six of us. I sit crossed-legged alongside my father on the west side of the

blanket. My mother sits to the north, separated from my father by my younger brother, Tom, who is lying across my mother's outstretched legs. He is five years younger than me and rarely leaves my mother's side. It is almost as if he cannot function without some part of his body touching hers. My father says it is unnatural behaviour for a seven year old. My mother seems to like it. She props herself up with two straightened arms outstretched behind her.

Opposite me sits my gramma. The distance between her and the large wicker picnic basket suggests she is unduly worried that somebody may steal it or, worse still, open it without her say-so. Next to her (and thus next to me) at the south end of the picnic sits Gramps. His back is slightly turned to me, his brown polished shoes just encroaching on the blanket. He is wearing a full three-piece suit and tie. Sweat from his grey temples glistens in the sunshine.

"Are we actually going to eat today?" he barks, his question landing somewhere centrally between us all.

Gramma smiles warmly and begins unpacking the basket. Paper plates, plastic cups, knives and forks and all manner of items begin a circle from my gramma to my mother and so on, until I pass each item to my gramps. He doesn't acknowledge me, and instead of holding items up until my wrists hurt, I place his items in a small pile between us.

Gramma removes from the basket plates and bowls full of food, all held in place with tight cling film on which condensation has formed. Everything is spread out on the blanket in front of us: an array of sandwiches, sausage rolls, tomatoes, lettuce, vol-au-vents, crisps, celery, cheese, crackers. We wait patiently as she removes the cling film from each item. Gramps lights his pipe and we all wait a little longer until he has finished smoking. I watch the smoke disappear into the blue sky and wish for a moment it was me.

Eventually, Gramps collects his plate and begins to fill it with food. Again, we all wait, watching in silence until he has finished. Then he places his plate down on the grass next to him and bows his head solemnly. He closes his eyes and reopens them, and that is an indication that we can now join in.

I watch as Gramma fusses around, passing plates crammed with different food to each of us so we can fill our plates with what we wish. To break the silence, she insists on describing what is on each plate as we take it from her. My mother fills her own plate and one for my brother. She encourages him to sit up to eat. I notice her touch my gramma's hand and their eyes make contact for the shortest time. Then she pours diluted orange juice into the plastic cups that we each hold out. Except for Gramps.

I am about to bite into my sausage roll when I see my father's brow crease. He nods to divert my attention to Gramma, who at last is able to collect

her own food from what is left. I place the sausage roll back on my plate and wait.

To my right, I hear Gramps chewing his food loudly. His teeth crunch and gnaw each mouthful as if there is a time limit until the food permanently disappears. I suppose in some ways it is. I hear the saliva clack-clacking between his cheeks and gums, in the spaces where his teeth used to be. I imagine tiny pieces of carrot being thrown from the top to the bottom of his mouth and back again, twisting and spinning on saliva rapids. I imagine it's like being in a kayak or on a waterslide.

He discards his empty plate, which lands on top of a bowl of luminous-orange cheesy crisps. He then lies back on the grass and places his cap over his face, exposing only his mouth, which turns down at the edges.

"Did you enjoy that, dear?" Gramma asks him.

"No. Too wet. Should've used foil."

I watch as Gramma smiles uneasily, her eyes flicking around all sides of the compass. Then she picks up a tomato, and I take my sausage roll and put it in my mouth just as she takes her first bite of the tomato. The silence is almost palpable, an invisible ghost that hovers above the blanket. I push food into my mouth, chewing as quietly as the scene around me. I'm not sure why we are all eating in silence. I suspect it is because Gramps is being silent. I chew on a small pork pie and realise that I am doing so in tandem with Gramps' chest inflating and emptying.

My father stretches and places his plate on the edge of the picnic blanket. A small gust of wind collects it and deposits it, upside down, in the salad bowl. He shrugs, perhaps to himself, and then lies back on the grass. His eyes are hidden by the crook of his elbow. His mouth reminds me of Gramps'.

Gramma nods and winks at me as she sucks on a mouthful of crisps. She looks grey. Grey and solemn. Her eyes remind me of the prisoners and refugees I have seen on the news. Eyes don't seem to shine when the hope is taken from them.

I notice a similar look on my mother's face. Her eyes crease when she sees me looking at her and a shy smile crosses her lips. I smile back broadly.

"What are you smiling at?" Tom asks loudly.

Gramma's head snaps toward him.

"Mum," I say quietly, hoping that Tom will take the volume hint (though he could be forgiven for his loud voice on the basis that he is in an expansive park full of hundreds if not thousands of people).

He doesn't. "Mum, Sam is pulling faces at me."

Mum frowns at me.

"Samuel," my father snaps.

Tom smirks.

I decide not to protest.

"So," says Gramma almost inaudibly, "any plans for this week, Sandra?"

"Not really," Mum says. There is a nervousness in her smile.

"Oh," says Gramma.

And then I am returned to the present. Completely aware of life around me. Suddenly, colours and sounds cascade from all directions. I hear the shouts of excitable children and the sound of bats hitting balls and, I hear laughter.

Laughter.

The ghost lifts from above the blanket, disappearing into the sky like chimney smoke. I see the brightness of the world come swiftly into focus. I see people smiling, running, talking. I see dogs eagerly taking in their surroundings, sniffing at trees, their tongues hanging in the summer heat.

I see enjoyment.

I look around our blanket again. Tom has rested back on my mother's knees and she is playing idly with his hair as she stares above my shoulder and into space. Something tells me that she hasn't noticed the colours like I have. Dad and Gramps are breathing in warm air whilst dreaming about anything but the picnic. Gramma begins emptying half-eaten bowls of food into one another. Celery with tomatoes. Damp sausage rolls alongside cheese-and-pineapple sticks. Unfinished vol-au-vents crammed in with strategically broken breadsticks. And then our picnic blanket is empty.

Just like our picnic.

Empty.

Empty of enjoyment. It's like a huge handful of happiness was sprinkled onto the park from above and somehow missed our blanket. Missed my family.

I lie back and let the summer sun warm my face, happy for one reason alone. That this event happens but once a year.

Chapter 3

It is the sound of my phone vibrating that wakes me from the dream about my mother and a picnic that happened almost exactly twenty-five years ago. I have had the same dream so many times that I have been able to pinpoint every moment of the day that the final picnic took place. In some ways it was easy to do. After all, I never saw my mother again after that day. You don't forget the details of days as significant as that.

I roll over to my right and watch the phone progress slowly over the edge of the bedside table. It swings for a moment, attached to its charging cable, and then hangs precariously like a mountaineer over a precipice.

I retrieve the still-vibrating phone and lie on my back. I push the button on the side and note that the caller is my father.

I could do without this.

The green circle allows me to answer, and am immediately greeted by the usual recorded message. I press '1' to accept and there are numerous clicks before his voice breaks through.

"Sam?" he says.

"Hi, Dad."

"How are you, son?"

"I'm good," I say. "And you?"

"Yeah. Y'know. I'm okay. Considering."

"Good."

Our conversations have always been much the same and now, in the position we both find ourselves, I have little hope that this will ever change. Even in the past — before my mother vanished — my father always kept our exchanges (and those with most other people) as short as possible. Our conversations almost exclusively serve as a way for my father to obtain information rather than share it. Today is different.

"Listen," he says, "your gramma hasn't got long left."

"Okay," I say, and before I can speak again, he interrupts my pause.

"Let's not pretend it matters to you," he says, quite rightly. "But she has no-one close, and well —"

It's my turn to interrupt. "So you think I should go and see her?"

"I'd do it myself..." he says. Neither of us feel the need to end his sentence. We both know why he can't. Doesn't.

My mind jumps to Tom.

My father tells me where my gramma is, which turns out to be only a mile or so from my home. You see, I was the one who stayed back. I was the

one who stayed marooned in a broken town full of broken memories. Just in case Mum reappeared. You never know.

It seems that Gramma stayed too. But I didn't know that. I haven't spoken to her since I was eighteen. And that was nineteen years ago.

"So you will?" my father says.

"Dunno. Maybe," I say, the vagueness sounding far better in my head. It's my attempt at taking a little control back. If you had listened carefully you would have heard an uncertain tremor in my delivery.

"I suggest you do," he says in a voice which suggests there may be ramifications if I choose not to.

My only remaining thread of control is severed when he hangs up the phone. I take a deep breath and wait for him to call back, which is something he does when he feels he may not have made his point as clearly as he might. I lay there staring at the dust that has collected in the corners of my phone. The screen stays black, and after a minute or two passes I feel safe again. I place the phone on the duvet and turn my face into the darkness of the pillow.

For a moment I am gripped by anger, a feeling that twists in my chest like a coiled rope. I have spent a good part of the last ten years trying to remove this feeling from my life. I have been told on a number of occasions that if I cannot leave it

behind, it will eventually consume me. I'll be tossed into the black hole of its throat like Jonah and his whale. Gobbled up in one. My final resting place will be the belly of the giant beast and, unlike Jonah, I'll never be seen again.

The last person who told me this was Sara. In fact, she told me plenty of times that I needed to change aspects of myself. For some time I listened to her, convinced that my macabre back story was reason enough to be the person I've become. It was only latterly, when I had an awakening, that I realised that her criticisms of me were actually a product of her own insecurities. Her insecurities moulding me into an angry and self-pitying person. A person I never used to be, nor ever wanted to be. And so, over the last year or so, the words I had listened to so attentively were rubberised and deflected, unheard, back to where they came from. And of course, as I am sure you can now guess,

Sara is gone.

And I feel the real me returning.

Slowly.

"NOTHING IS AS IT SEEMS..."

NOW TURN THE BOOK AND READ ON
FROM PAGE 16...